Introduction

IN THIS edition we delve into the profound theme of honor. As writers and readers, we are continually drawn to the concept of honor. Not merely as a personal virtue but as a mirror reflecting our collective values, struggles, and aspirations. In a world often marked by upheaval and ambiguity, honor remains a steadfast anchor, guiding actions, shaping identities, and inspiring stories that resonate across time and cultures.

Honor is both a personal code and a societal contract. It manifests in acts of integrity, courage, humility, and sacrifice. It challenges us to uphold what is right, even when it is difficult, and to live authentically in accordance with our deepest convictions.

Literature has long been a vessel for examining what it means to be honorable. From the valorous deeds of epic heroes to the quiet dignity of everyday lives, writers have used their craft to probe the moral fabric that binds us. In these stories, poems, and essays, we see honor tested by adversity, redefined by cultural shifts, and challenged by moral dilemmas. It is in these moments of tension and reflection that literature reveals its power: to elevate virtue, expose hypocrisy, and inspire change.

As you journey through this issue, we encourage you to consider how honor shapes your own understanding of integrity and reputation. How do societal expectations influence our perceptions of honor? How do people manage situations where the requirements of personal integrity and community loyalty differ? And in a world where honor can be both a shield and a burden, what stories do we tell about the pursuit of true virtue?

Empyrean *Autumn 2025*

A QUARTERLY OF ARTS AND LITERATURE
PUBLISHED INDEPENDENTLY

Editor-in-Chief
Kaylyn Dunn

Sponsored by
Kada's Bookstore

Special Additions by
Isabella Ballew
Mel Einhorn
Lena N. Gemmer

https://www.empyreanliterarymagazine.com/

To submit, go to:
www.empyreanliterarymagazine.com/generalsubmissions

Contents

ISSUE 15: VOL. 4, NO. 3

Growing Pains

1st Place Fiction Winner   Isabella Ballew

When we were little, we used to run around in tall grasses, hawk-eyed for specs of yellow hidden in the morning dew. The satisfying squish of ladybug eggs under a coarse rock was the only treatment for the chronic restlessness of childhood. We didn't mind the heat back then, unconcerned with sweat stains; we explored relentlessly, stopping only to pant like dogs under a particularly shady tree or feel the cool press of a ribbed water bottle against the backs of our necks. Over the years, as our activities grew bolder and more fully-formed, I would find myself chasing those fleeting moments of hyperactivity in the pounding summer sun.

A small group of us, congregating mostly around Holleybrooke Road, by virtue of our nearest school bus stop, were intent on passing our summer as delinquently as possible. Our forays into amateur criminality began small, as we were chased out of Mrs. Bennett's gardens for stealing from her delicately tended strawberry bushes. Our budding reputation as kids 'up to no good' preceded us– Mrs. Bennett made quick work of passing along our antics to any neighbor or parent who would listen. Our group's commonality was clear: our parents had abandoned us to wreak havoc upon our neighborhood. As the latchkey kids of dual-earning families, we had been largely left to our own devices. So with the impending feeling of a summer soon ending, we sought to ramp up our antics before our burgeoning, doomed athletics careers and remedial after-school math classes gave new purpose to our aimlessness.

Our group's lineup was in constant mutation but largely consisted of founding members– twins Greg and Owen Smith, their friend Tyler, my neighbor Miguel, quiet but ever-present Austin, and me. We had all independently found our way to wandering around the neighborhood, and fused almost as unintentionally. One night after consuming an unreasonable amount of frozen fish sticks and powdered lemonade, I searched for 'the guys' and found them standing outside the woods at the south side of the subdivision's edge. Through the clearing, I could make out an overgrown stone path careening deeper into the forest. Owen –the group's prodigal leader– made the first motions, followed closely behind by his twin shadow, and then Tyler and Miguel, who feigned flippant disinterest despite Tyler's raging cowardice. He would sooner piss himself out of fear rather than diverge from the Smith twins' intentions. Austin and I trailed in the back –at least consistently fainthearted– not wanting to be the newest targets of the Smiths' merciless teasing tactics. They were the youngest of five, and calculated insults were as much their hand-me-downs as their matching oversized tartan flannels.

I grasped the bottom of Austin's lime green tie-dyed Vacation Bible School shirt with the veracity of somebody who had not yet ruled out the possibility of ghouls. I tried to ignore the thick brush of forest steadily blocking out the late afternoon light. He continued without protest, leading us behind the other boys, in step.

After what could have been minutes or hours of venturing into the woods, we emerged in a small clearing. While no longer dense forest, the clearing was covered in brush and overgrown vegetation – wildflowers interspersed the reeds– creating a rainbow moat of petals around a rusty chain link fence. I looked down at the purple and yellow hues and flicked away a meandering tick that had been crawling up my leg. A crumbling wooden house stood firmly within the fenced area, at war with its surroundings, a losing battle of age and decay.

"C'mon, let's go in," Owen said with the decisive bravado that commonly carried his hare-brained schemes.

"Absolutely not," I protested in my winy timbre before he completed his thought. He narrowed his eyes at me, and I let the edge of Austin's shirt fall.

"If you're going to be a pussy about it, why don't you just go home?" he asked, as I quickly withered under his glare. I thought of the emptiness typical of my house in early evening, the whirring sounds of the refrigerator just barely audible under the muffled voice of a news anchor blaring in the direction of my sleeping mother, who had likely collapsed on the couch after another sixteen-hour shift as a trauma nurse. My father, a long-haul trucker, usually graced us with his presence biannually, preferring to present as a consistent monthly check to keep the lights on and the pantry full. Without a sibling or pet, and unable to so much as turn the channel without facing the wrath of unearthing my mother from her slumber in our 380 sq. ft cottage, I generally avoided home until just before bed.

Now, I look back at these moments under the clarity of adulthood and laugh at my futile desperation to be included in spaces I didn't fit within- a feverous persistence at shoving a square peg into a round hole and the same incredulous reaction when it didn't slide in with ease. My desperation, while humiliating, held the power of somebody who had not yet felt the true weight of everything society would not let her accomplish.

"It is getting pretty late." Tyler interrupted, and for once, I was grateful for his spinelessness. Tyler had long made an enemy of me through both his incessant whining and obsequious nature toward the twins. My opinion was overridden by said twins, who, while impartial to his brown-nosing, upon hearing that Tyler had not only Pokémon Stadium but Tony Hawk's Pro Skater as well, welcomed him into the group with open arms. Finding a parent willing to purchase us games was rare; my parents were rarely willing to buy much more than a six-pack of beer for themselves and a Happy Meal for you, if you played your cards right.

"I'm sorry, I didn't realize you were *all* a bunch of girls," echoed Greg, unsurprisingly. His opinions hardly differed from Owens, both so used to operating in unison, the only apparent difference was a barely perceptible scar in the middle of Greg's forehead, between his eyebrows. The mark had been the gift of Greg running obediently headfirst into a banister at the behest of one of his older brothers, who often used the twins as entertainment. It was somewhat comforting to know their dictatorial leanings were playing out in turn against them in their own home, where they had initially learned these skills.

I struggled to shield my reaction, feeling my blood boil at being reduced to a descriptor of weakness. I looked to the others for support and found nothing– my only real ally, Austin, was sensitive but didn't have the guts to counter the twins. Austin was a lanky boy with a bowl haircut who moved into the neighborhood sometime in the summer of 2000. He had moved to Holleybrooke most recently and still found himself mildly bullied for the length of his socks and the vivid, deep blue of his jeans. It seemed like every week a new family would move into the rapidly multiplying single household developments that cropped up relentlessly up and down Holleybrooke Road's branching streets. We would circle their cul-de-sacs hollering on our bikes, waiting for some poor unsuspecting soul to join us.

In the twins, Austin had found solace; he could withstand their commentary as long as they included him. The twins didn't mind who joined as long as they pulled their weight– they didn't often question anyone's contribution except mine. As an only child who had moved into the much nicer, newer additions to our neighborhood, Austin's basement was always available when we needed an air-conditioned reprieve from the sun. While I knew he would apologize later –likely with the peace offering of half of a Kit Kat bar– I couldn't help the disappointment for the lack of support.

Miguel offered even less assistance; he hungered for adventure in ways that existed outside of typical childhood rebellion, and I often caught him looking with great interest at the house beyond the fence. He lingered back patiently while we argued, running a broken branch against the length of the chain link fence, the repetitive clacking as he pulled it against the chain links was a rather faithful sonic recreation of a spin-the-wheel game. The sound echoed through the clearing.

I felt my role in the group was called into question. What reason did they have to include me if they all saw me as *just a girl*? I was allegedly a beacon of fearfulness who lacked tenacity. With renewed fervor brought on by resentment, the questionable existence of spirits left my mind as I propelled myself toward the fence with a running start. The gate had been locked with multiple padlocks, so I bypassed the entrance entirely. My feet were small enough to stick into the openings, and my arms were strong enough –from almost half a decade of scaling the overgrown oak behind my family home– to hoist myself over. I found myself over the fence intact, save for a few scratches on the inside of my forearm. I looked back towards the boys with my arms crossed, a dare etched into my expression– *are you coming or what?*

The twins smiled and made quick work of the fence themselves. My bravery earned me a clap on the back from Owen; I chagrin to admit the swell of pride it roused in me. As hubristic as they were, they couldn't hold a candle to me in any feat of physical prowess. Miguel went over the fence with similar ease and helped lift Tyler over the final barbs at the top. Austin attempted to scale the fence a few times but had neither the strength to lift himself over the top nor the speed to run and vault it like I did. I saw the embarrassment in the red of his cheeks, but kept mute in silent retaliation for his lack of support.

"Keep watch!" Owen yelled back at him, and Austin slumped down onto the ground with his back facing the fence.

Much of my fear had been replaced by adrenaline, and I allowed myself to take in my surroundings. The outside of the house was a gray slatted wood that was in the process of being eaten away by termites. One side of the house had been sprayed by a large red 'A' breaking through a similarly scrawled circle surrounding it. Numerous beer cans spilled their way onto the lawn from the wide-open front door and its caved-in frame. I ventured inside to see that the barren concrete floor was littered with extinguished votives.

We circled the ground floor in awe until I noticed Miguel climbing the half-disintegrated staircase on the far side of what was once an expansive living room. He used the wall as leverage to creep along the side that was still intact and soon disappeared over the top of the stairs. We heard his voice– a distant beacon,

"You guys gotta come check this out, there's some really cool old stuff up here." Greg and Owen seemed indifferent to the prospect of old relics, and Tyler was glued to the side of the wall in terror of apparitions or perhaps teenagers– at that age, both prospects were equally frightening. I was moved by a budding anthropological sense to make the most of the opportunity and crept up the stairs by mimicking Miguel's previous path. The promised treasure was even greater than I had imagined; the contents of someone's life had been time-capsuled in this attic for – in comparison to my meager eleven years– what appeared as an eternity. I found a cardboard box filled with old National

Geographics and checked the date stamped on each cover: 1971, 1972, and so on. Aside from the magazines, many boxes included the contents of personal belongings, from nightgowns to old family photographs. I got the sense that whoever had initially left these things had intended to come back for them. Any guilt I might have felt for prying into someone's private things was washed away by sheer curiosity, and I found myself bent down rifling through the boxes. My eyes were caught by a plastic pen encased in a smiling hot pink dinosaur with lime green scales. It was covered in a fine layer of dirt, but I couldn't help slipping it into my pocket- a keepsake of our adventure. I began flipping through the old magazines and became so engrossed in *Thor Heyerdahl's Own Story of The Voyage of Ra II* and the voyage of Kon-Tiki, I barely noticed Miguel had quietly slipped back downstairs.

"Come on, Cassie, I have to get back for dinner!" Miguel shouted from below. Knowing how upset Mrs. Flores became when Miguel arrived too late, I crossed the room back towards the staircase quickly. Or rather, I began to- until suddenly I was opening my eyes, looking up at the ceiling. The next few moments I experienced in a fog of semi-perception; now, in retrospect, the event sits even less clearly in my memories.

Duplicate blonde faces peered down at me with expressions contorted halfway between horror and worry. I noticed another grimacing face in the corner of my eye –though my vision was blurry– as Tyler wailed, with tears and snot streaming down his face in cascading rivers. I could hardly hear him cry over the sound of ringing in my ears. Above me,

I could just make out what looked like a jagged human-sized hole in the ceiling.

I tried to sit up but felt hands pressing down on my shoulders; sounds began to regain clarity, but were garbled and far away.

"You're going to be okay, Cassie. Miguel ran to get help!

Please don't move,
Please don't move,
Please don't move."

I shifted as much as possible and felt the dinosaur pen poking into my hip from my pocket as I craned my neck up to attempt to take in my surroundings. The next sight was jarring in ways I hadn't been prepared for. Where I expected to see two straight legs stretched in front of me, I instead saw a glimpse of the white of bone poking out through an unnatural angle and a spattering of blood soaking into my favorite jeans. A wave of nausea propelled through me, wrapping itself in panic until darkness overtook me.

***

My leg took over 6 months to heal. My mother took to sleeping on the couch while I was given her luxurious queen-sized master bed for my recovery time. Numerous surgeries had introduced a series of metal rods and screws to my constitution, each of which needed special attention in my healing process. Unable to move on my own, I found myself parked in front of the small box TV watching hours and hours of Rugrats and other shows geared for much younger children– as was typical of daytime programming. I distracted myself

15

as often as possible in the early weeks of my recovery; it was the only real salve for the unbearable throbbing pain that would ebb and flow throughout all hours, often even waking me in the middle of the night. I found my sleep schedule shifted to adapt to witness more interesting television, and found solace in *Malcolm in the Middle* and *The Fresh Prince of Bel-Air*; lulled by the canned laughter of their studio audience. Sometimes I would break up the days of television with attempts at reading, although initially I was put off by my short attention span and lack of useful vocabulary. By the end of my recovery, however, I had jumped multiple reading levels and felt myself pulled towards the daring and twisted fantasies of Tolkien and Le Guin. Every other week, I made Austin go on large-scale library runs, watching through the window as he rode up, balancing stacks of books in the small basket in front of his bike.

Austin was, in fact, the primary visitor who graced my home during my months of recovery. He would come by regularly to drop off more books and stay to watch television or let me play his brand new Gameboy Advance. We had become much closer through his consistent appearances; I appreciated not having to take on this ordeal in complete solitary confinement. He would come over to patiently watch me virtually struggle for twenty minutes to jump onto a platform or be murdered over and over again by the same mushroom man with only minimal commentary and an insistence that I call them Goombas and not "angry mushrooms." He would devolve into laughter at the sight of my labored, single-legged bouncing to reach something a foot across the room. He was also my only direct line of contact back to our little world.

School had restarted while I was still bedridden, and I tried to maintain my assignments at home. The sixth grade brought on more difficult coursework, and despite all my newfound free time, without the in-person instruction, I was struggling to keep up. He told me diligently about how the Smiths had joined the football team and rarely went out of their way to talk to any of us neighborhood kids anymore. Tyler had attempted to sit with them at lunch and was almost completely ignored, so he had shifted into spending more time with Austin. Miguel came by often enough, as my neighbor, he had the greatest ease of access, though he never lingered too long. I was eternally grateful whenever he brought leftovers of his mom's delicious cooking, and I had a momentary respite from microwaved Hungry-Man for breakfast, lunch, and dinner.

Socially, in middle school, six months felt like an eternity, and the unnerving shift of friendship dynamics rattled me; I had little input on my changing role in the complicated ecosystem. I felt a general uneasiness about the prospect of re-entering halfway through the year. Although I had gone to school with most of these kids since early childhood, they all felt foreign to me. My isolation had taken a toll on my development, and I felt unmoored by my newfound social anxiety.

A month before I was cleared to have my cast removed and walk on my own, I practiced standing in my mother's bedroom, propped up by Austin on one side and my mom on the other. Too distracted to focus on the joy of being vertical after so long, I was perplexed at how high I now had to crane my neck to see Austin's face. So much had changed in my absence.

The day they removed my cast was surprisingly uneventful, aside from seeing what had become of my leg since its imprisonment. My mother drove me to the same hospital, with Austin in tow in the backseat for moral support. Through lack of muscle use, my leg had withered away to half its previous size, and the ghostly pale and atrophied appendage felt like a foreign object. The hair underneath the cast had grown long and darker than before, and I suddenly felt embarrassed to have my friend witness this moment. We drove back in silence, as Austin was usually sensitive to my moods. While I initially expected a feeling of overwhelming joy at the removal of my cast, I felt distracted by the overbearing weight of anxiety upon re-entering society.

***

We all erupted with a squeal as my friend's older sister hit a large pothole in the road. We were jumbled in the backseat, on the way to some high school junior's party while his parents were out of town. As freshmen, we wore this as a badge of honor– to be attractive and interesting enough to warrant an invitation to a party of this caliber was nothing short of monumental, and would chart the course for the rest of our *high school experience*. This sentiment was proposed by Claire and even more realistically passed down to us by her older sister.

"You look so hot!" Claire's sister exclaimed as she caked my eyes in thick liner. I felt the weight of

the makeup like a sack of bricks- making it difficult
to keep my eyes open. The unsaid *unlike usual* hung
heavy in the air between us.

I felt wary but tried to stay in character– I had
borrowed her mini shorts that said ALL NIGHTER
on the back in glittering pink rhinestones and the
tightest pink camisole I owned over a borrowed
push-up bra. I attempted to ignore the cavernous
gaps between cloth and intention, as Claire said that
the inclusion of us at these kinds of events would be
contingent on our ability to *show up and show out*.
So with that, Claire, Madison, Becca, and I donned
our costumes and threw ourselves in the back of her
older sister's car. The passenger seat had been taken
by her sister's boyfriend, an older-looking man with
a star neck tattoo who refused to close the window
at the insistence that he needed to be constantly
smoking cigarettes. The car smelled similar to the
weeks when my dad was home, and I tried holding
my nose to keep from gagging at the smell. My
attempts to adapt to the social expectations were
labored, far more difficult than my ill-forgotten
tomboy era.

My nerves about re-entering the arena of *school*
after my accident in the summer before sixth grade
had me in a crippling panic, but luckily, I was
assigned to sit next to Claire in Homeroom Class.
With my adoption, I was immediately tossed into a
crash course in girl world and all its expected
behaviors. Beyond that, I was equally thrust into her
long-term friend group. What I lacked in common
interest with them, I was eternally grateful to not be
eating lunch alone. I had somehow avoided the
predictable, isolated experience of being the odd
one out and had instead slightly molded myself into

being somebody who could be tolerated by this group of girls. I had built a profound respect for Claire and her ability to wield her magnetism to her benefit –although they watched too many reruns of *Friends*– and I had adapted in turn. Middle school had introduced block lunch periods, and I found myself separated from Austin and Tyler. I still saw them around the neighborhood and on some weekends but found that I needed to forge my path in the interim. Claire liked me because, in her own words, 'I kept it real,' which I interpreted as the fact that they primarily kept me around to revel in my discomfort with femininity, as some long-form endeavor in comic relief.

Claire's sister parked her car in a random field, and we all endured the march to the party house. The area was more affluent than anything I was used to; the richest people I knew growing up had petite bungalows that paled in comparison with the monstrosities before my eyes. Multi-level mansions stretched out in farcical patterns, presenting the baffling idea that somebody could own gyms and pools and not have to clip the scholastic coupons off every cereal box at the potential promise of discounted school supplies. I followed Claire and the other girls in search of familiar faces until we stopped by the kitchen bar's various assortments of flavored vodkas –some kept in labeled water bottles, mysteriously acquired– and sodas. I was halfway through watching Claire tepidly create a lime green concoction of Mtn Dew and peach flavored SKYY when I spotted a familiar face through the sliding screen doors.

I bounded up without hesitation and threw my arms around my most familiar friend.

"What the hell are you doing here?" I asked, shocked not only that Austin was at this party, but at any party at all. Austin spent most of his time gaming in his room and scrolling on 4chan. I knew very little about what his strange favorite website entailed, but having accidentally glanced at one too many gruesome cartoon images consisting of stick figures and slurs, I dared not inquire further. I simply knew that the kind of kids who spent so much time killing time didn't often end up in parties like this, and felt grateful for a comforting presence.

Austin motioned toward a few people in the corner with his head, "Twins brought me."

At the beginning of eighth grade, Owen had been found with a small amount of weed in the locker room, hidden in his deodorant stick. Due to the school's zero-tolerance policy on drugs, he had been immediately kicked off the football team and expelled. Greg, seemingly unable to exist as an independent human, followed and also transferred to a charter school still in our district. I had heard all of this secondhand from Austin, as the accident had somewhat soured me to being in their company. My time was filled by hanging out with Claire and being in the yearbook club; as such, my neighborhood wanderings had all but ceased. I felt a pang of resentful envy toward Greg and Owen's flippant tossing off of their football endeavors. Before the accident, I might have joined track or continued playing softball. Unfortunately, my leg never fully recovered enough to compete in sports, and I even felt pain when walking long distances.

"Yo, whoa is that Cassie dude?" Owen said, walking up to where Austin and I were speaking.

"Yeah," I answered curtly, already having had enough of the conversation.

"Cass, you look like a total smoke show," Greg said, walking up to join his brother in the conversation.

"You look like a raccoon," Austin tacked on, and coming from anybody else, I might have been offended, but I could sense Austin knew how uncomfortable I felt and was trying to lighten the mood.

"Bite like one too." I countered, deadpan. Austin smiled while the twins looked perplexed.

Just then, Claire and the other girls walked up as well, "Oh my god, Cassie, how rude you didn't introduce us to your cute friends." She batted her eyelashes a few times in recurrence. I rolled my eyes in response. Claire flirted for sport, and I had a feeling the Smith twins were about to become sounding boards for her practice session. Madison whispered in my ear, "The dark-haired one is so cute." I followed her gaze to Tyler in the corner, who had finally had a growth spurt and ended up the kind of conventionally attractive that girls like Madison would find "cute." I tried not to burst out laughing at the idea of sniveling little Tyler being cute, but he had changed, and I figured I ought not hold it against him. In what now seemed like a childhood reunion, I couldn't help noticing Miguel's absence.

"You guys still see Miguel?" I asked, knowing full well they didn't, but wanting to antagonize them. Miguel was still my neighbor, so I saw him and his family occasionally. I had already received the details on the disillusionment of his friendship with the Smiths. Commentary from a football friend of Greg and Owen's had severed their nine-year friendship last July. Politics and racial divides were no longer rendered null; the era of freely uniting over a desire to run around was long gone. The blissful ignorance of childhood had passed, the divides of society bearing on all of our friendships in full.

"Nah, he's too cool for us now," Owen responded with a smile.

"Interesting," I said, meaning anything but. I let the conversation shift to be between the guys I had grown up with and the girls I now spent most of my time with. Sure of the fact that Claire could handle herself and was having fun, I extricated myself from the conversation, pulling Austin with me. We played a few games of beer pong and people-watched the crowd.

"I bet the only band on his iTunes library is the Red Hot Chili Peppers," he said, pointing to a guy in a backwards cap taking a large rip from a fluorescent blue bong on full display in the living room.

"I bet she's going to grow up to be a real estate agent," I said, pointing to a girl wearing a business casual top and pinstripe pants with a thick chunky necklace. We burst out into laughter. Austin's expression turned serious,

"Hey, I have to tell you something."

"Okay, shoot." I had a light buzz going, and being inexperienced with drinking felt myself feeling buzzy and lightheaded.

"My dad got a new job."

"Well, tell Mr. Warren congratulations from me," I said overly-enthusiastically, causing Austin to smile. I had always gotten along with his parents.

I appreciated how they were physically present in ways mine could not be.

"He's making a lot more money."

"More money? How could it be humanly possible to make more money than your parents? You have a basement! A driveway!" *Your dad drives a Mercedes.*

"You have a driveway," Austin said, giving me a side eye, tone defensive.

"No, we have a dirt path my mom drove over so many times the grass all died." I knew Austin felt insecure about being relatively wealthy, but I couldn't help feeling annoyed that he thought we were living similarly.

"Anyway, my parents have been feeling kind of cramped in our house, so they bought another one. They're going to let me finish out the year, and then we're moving to Riverwood."

The buzzing feeling increased steadily, and I felt a sense of panic. I managed to spit out a response. "Riverwood! Whoa, that's so far."

A full thirty minutes closer to the city, Riverwood was an affluent neighborhood primarily known for some of its B-list celebrity residents, and most people traveled in golf carts. Knowing how unlikely I was to catch a ride given my mother's hours, I knew I wouldn't be making it to Riverwood anytime soon. We sat in silence for a while, letting that knowledge sink in.

"Shit." I finally said.

"Shit," he echoed.

Since the accident, Austin had become my closest friend, and although lately we had been spending slightly less time together, he felt integral to my existence. The alcohol, in combination with my inexperience at consuming it, had made my head feel heavy, so I leaned on his shoulder, desperately wishing I could keep my best friend in that exact location. I felt my thoughts drift for a moment before I felt his hand rubbing circles on my back, and I stilled. The gesture seemed strangely intimate, and I tried to subtly scoot further away. Whenever Austin and I had touched in the past, whether it be a playful shove or hug, it had always felt deeply platonic. Tonight, something about his touch felt different; the pressure with which he curled his finger as he moved up to my shoulder felt possessive and lacked the gentle quality with which he usually maneuvered. I avoided looking at his eyes, somewhat scared of the expression I might find.

I suddenly felt a swift and hard object hit the back of my head, saving me.

"My bad, dudes. Aimed too wide." I looked over at Tyler, collecting a football he had tossed at Greg.

My head felt fine, but I used the opportunity to disrupt the moment, "Ugh, yeah, I'm going to go get some ice."

I saw Austin look at me with concern, "I can grab some."

"Don't worry about it," I waved him off. "I need to make sure Claire and the other girls don't leave me." With my explanation secured, I all but ran inside the house, darting around to find Claire.

An hour later, I found myself in a pile of sleeping bags with the girls, demolishing boxes of chicken nuggets picked up from McDonald's on our way home. I thought about telling them what had happened. Claire seemed like a mentor for boy advice. However, as much as she liked to flirt, I equally knew she had little tangible experience. I left the moment unsaid, hoping with some small kernel of hope that if I never spoke it aloud, it meant it never happened.

***

At the end of my final year of high school, Facebook began to take off, and I remember receiving floods of friend requests from people who had been in my life previously. After logging in on one random Tuesday, I audibly gasped while looking at the screen at the library desktop I frequented on the off day I did my homework. 1 New Friend Request. Austin Warren.

I accepted immediately and started scrolling through the photos and posts on his profile. He looked older, and somehow -impossibly- taller. I wasn't sure who his new friends were, but they had influenced his style. His signature bright blue denim had turned to black, His hair swooped to the side at an impossible angle, and he appeared to have gotten his lip pierced. I remember how he'd gone on and on about not understanding why people would ruin their faces by putting holes in them –likely echoing his parents' opinions– I hadn't agreed, but I'd marked it off as a facet of his character. I suppose he felt differently now.

I felt a pang of sadness, remembering. I had been so nervous about that strange moment between us, I had distanced myself unconsciously; it felt inevitable somehow, with his move, that things would have to move on. I assumed he had been drunk and unaware, or that if he had harbored some secret feelings for me, I would receive some sort of confession, despite having no interest in changing the conditions of our friendship. Yet, it was as if the party never happened. He never brought it up, or even hinted that anything out of the ordinary had happened, so at a certain point I started to second-guess my memory. Maybe he had put a casual hand on my back, and in my drunken stupor, I incorrectly interpreted his signals?

After Austin moved to Riverwood, we'd kept up for a time, but both of us had busy schedules. My job at the movie theater ate up most of my time. We emailed a lot at first, talked on the phone, but the messages became farther and fewer in between. At some point last year, he just stopped responding. With college fast approaching, I never thought to reach back out, but finding his friend request felt serendipitous. I shot off a quick message.

Me: hey stranger 6:54 PM.

I worked on a final paper I had due for English in the interim, pausing every five minutes or so to quickly click over to the web browser and see if he responded. If I remembered anything still about Austin, I knew he played video games in his room after school, and I guessed his parents would have bought him a personal computer.

I finally saw a notification around 8:30 PM. *Austin Warren has poked you.* Poked me, what could that possibly mean? I sent him back a reply.

Me: …? 8:32 PM.

Austin: Haha 8:36 PM.

Me: How have you been? 8:37 PM.

Austin: p good 8:45 PM.

Me: p good??? We haven't talked in forever. How is Riverwood? How is your dad's new job? Are you doing finals right now? 8:47 PM.

Austin: new school is cool 8:55 PM.

My heart sank in my chest, his messages had lost their usual length and tone, although Facebook was harder to read than email. I began to pack up my things; the library was closing in five minutes, and I still had a long bike ride home. Right before I logged off the library account, I received a final message from Austin.

Austin: Do you have a cell phone? 9:15 PM.

I thought about the new flip phone burning a hole in my pocket. I had saved up all my money from the movie theater to purchase it and felt pride at what I had earned. Still, I seldom texted on it because it was quite out of date, and typing out messages was much harder than on newer models. I sent my number anyway.

***

Austin's first message came early the next day and sounded closer to his old self. He updated me on his parents, new school, and new friends. He had delved headfirst into music interests and started playing the guitar. He seldom played video games anymore. Whatever cloying nostalgia I had for the past aside, I began enjoying communicating with my old friend. Even after we had caught up, I found myself texting him randomly throughout the day.

Me: Do you remember when we convinced Tyler to prank call Mrs. Beckett and pretend to be Homeland Security? 2:42 PM.

28

Austin: OMG I thought she was going to wrap her house in tinfoil 2:50 PM.

Talking to him brought a sense of ease to my days, and other than Claire, I felt like I held no similarly close relationships. The prospect of having Austin in my life again gave me renewed energy; the errant pain in my leg felt lighter even. I found myself occasionally reaching for the dinosaur pen I hadn't used in years that I kept at my bedside, bending around its plastic arms and legs into fun shapes while I waited for Austin to text back.

The talking went on for a month or so until I found myself in bed on a random Friday night, unable to sleep due to the stress of applying for financial aid for college next year. I had spent the entire evening rifling through old papers because my mother couldn't get off work to help me fill out the form. I texted Austin, hoping for some stress relief.

Me: Whatcha up to? 9:34 PM.
Austin: At a party! 9:50 PM.
Me: Oh, cool! Never mind then, I'll talk to you tomorrow. 9:55 PM.

I dove headfirst into a novel I had been reading, winding down for bed. A couple of hours later, just before I fell deep into sleep, I received another text from Austin. I opened the text and realized that it was an image. Since my phone was older, the image was slightly grainy, and I squinted in the dark to see what it was before the realization suddenly hit me.

Austin had sent me a picture of a penis. I laughed out loud, thinking at first it was some kind of internet gag and he would send a follow-up explanation. I waited for 10 minutes, then 20, and 30, but another text never came.

I found myself looking at it again, tilting my phone at an angle to examine the image from other angles- a brief foray into scientific examination. It dawned on me that what I was looking at was likely an image of Austin's dick. I found myself repulsed, not necessarily by the penis itself, which I regarded rather neutrally, as the manner in which it was presented gave an almost anatomical view. The angle of the shot had been taken closely enough that even with the blurry quality of my sub-rate phone, I could just make out the veins. My panic rose then, as I tried to explain it away, had it been an accident, meant for somebody else he was texting with? Something about the idea of Austin sending a picture of his penis to a girlfriend didn't sit quite right with me, but it made more sense than the alternative. Three hours had passed during my rumination, and I decided to send a follow-up text.

Me: Wrong number? 1:04 AM.
Austin: My dick is 10 inches 2:06 AM.

What was I supposed to do with this information? I was angry, the novel shock of being sent the image had worn off, replaced with a profound sadness in consideration of the state of our relationship. I found myself cyclically ruminating on the context of our relationship. Is this how my entrusted friend had viewed me all those years, reduced to an object of sexual desire, had our relationship meant nothing to him? Even if he had unrequited feelings, if he had brought it up during any conversation, would that not be a normal course of action? I started wondering if the sending of it unprompted had become some sort of sexual kink for him, and why then he had chosen me as the receiver?

The next morning, I waited for an explanation or apology that never came. Radiating silence plagued me throughout the day, and my mind wandered anxiously. Finally, when I was almost at my breaking point, I received a follow-up text.

Austin: Sup 4:06 PM.

Me: Sup !? 4:06 PM.

Austin: lol wut 4:10 PM.

Me: Is this like a thing for you? Is this something you do now? 4:12 PM.

Austin: sumtimes I had 2 do smthn our convo wasnt going anywhere 4:20 PM.

Me: What do you mean by not going anywhere? It's a conversation, it's just talking.

Why can't we just talk? 4:25 PM.

Austin: Tyler is my bff. I liked you. 4:30 PM.

Me: You never said anything. 4:31 PM.

Austin: You play too hard to get boo 4:45 PM.

I threw my phone across the room against my wall so hard that it shattered the back panel. I stare at the broken phone while light streams in through the window, reflecting off my tears.

#

An Uninvited Guest

1st Place Poetry Winner   Mel Einhorn

I sat with your mother's mother
Abandoned by those who claimed to be
Too brittle to keep her company
As she died in my arms
Cancer wreaked her intestines

After a summer
As a survival camp counselor
for disadvantaged children
With the putative sire
A powerless hulk in tow
You came home pregnant

Masked shoals of submerged choices
Preclude a call to action
"It's all my fault," you said
You chose to send him home
And legally declared yourself
Intent and on the way to college
As an emancipated minor
To be more loan-worthy
Asked, can you keep my room intact
As if it were a sanctuary

Ready as I was to stop
Cheating on everyone
And divorce your mother
Buried in a total disorder or ruined values
Untimely for me

My refugee parents I suppose
Could have tried harder
Provided more for me
Yet I respected that
They did their best
To come to terms
With what was
The Great Depression

I loved them
They loved me
Claimed poverty
They chose to deny life to my three aborted siblings
Not my place to judge

For you my daughter
In the shadow
Cast by my infidelity
Misled by entitlement
For you it might be easy
To be self-righteous
For me it is hard to contain
An instinct for vengeance

Dismayed not to be consulted
Before you and your mother opted for the abortion
I put aside though barely in my mind
The unremitted notion of
Grandparents raising your child
Which unconscionably
Might resurrect my presumed obligation
That of a captain on a sinking ship

My self-estranged daughter
You have become an uninvited guest
At a party to celebrate your birthday
You are the center of attention
Just what you want

Lost souls
We stay in touch
Long enough
To define lifelong roles
Responding like
A betrayed friend might
Without empathy

My parents deferred to me
As if I were a learned professor
Agreed to immediately bequeath their nest egg
savings
To my children
A symbolic gesture of sworn loyalty
Upon my promise that
I would pledge to maintain them
A legacy which you used later
To secure a rural property

My near fatal accidental distracted precipice plunge
Off a fast new racing bike
Left me with a fractured vertebra and a halfmoon
forehead gash
Long-term vertigo
Brought you to see me in the trauma center
Where you picked dried blood from my hair
A loving act which
Interrupted my desolation

You are the product of whimsical unprotected sex
We should have known better
A diehard romantic
Drawn to memorable daring
I was to blame
Not your mother
I forgave myself
Your mother spared me
From promulgating a despising family tradition
As I recalled
No one voiced the thought of
Voiding your existence

I loved you with my heart and soul
My self-estranged daughter
Now an uninvited guest
At an unattended party
To celebrate your birthday
Where you still
Are the center of attention
Just what you wanted

To second guess or malign you
With my rocky second half-life transition
Would've been hypocrisy
Sadly, you are a widow now living on a memorial
property
Seeded by my parents' generosity
With your pious mother, her Orthodox husband, a
caterer,
Who both tried to withhold my reciting
At your brother's synagogue confirmation service
Until your brother
With no prompting
Insisted or he wouldn't participate.

Even after I'd agreed
To a religious divorce release
For her to remarry compliant with the Orthodox
protocol

Our wedding was unlike yours
To an unheralded rock musician
In a country style facility
Near Woodstock
Which I borrowed money to fund

Our wedding lacked joy
With frenetic friends
The gaping Rabbi's mouth
Flapping Hebrew words
We were the first of our friends to marry
My poor boy's vision of
A detour wedding night
At Motel on the Mountain
A room on a platform
Embedded on a slope
A defiance of my fear of heights
And lost innocence

Whimsical unprotected sex with your virgin mother
We should have known better
A diehard romantic I was
Drawn to memorable daring
I forgave myself
Though your mother spared me
From considering with you
To kill an unborn child
A family tradition

My estranged daughter
You are an uninvited guest
At an unattended party to celebrate your birthday
Where you are the center of attention
Just what you wanted
A flower child widow now living in a memorial
property
With your pious mother, and her Orthodox husband,
a caterer,
Who tried to deny my attendance at your brother's
confirmation
Synagogue service until your brother insisted or he
wouldn't do it
Even after I'd agreed
To a religious divorce release
For her to remarry as an Orthodox Jew

Our wedding was unlike yours to a failed musician
At Woodstock
Which I borrowed money to fund
Our wedding lacked joy
With frenetic relatives
The gaping Rabbi's mouth
Flapping foreign words
The first of our friends to marry
At their own table
My poor boy's vision
A detour wedding night
At Motel of the Mountain
A platform room embedded on a slope

Defiance of my fear of heights
To upgrade the solemnity of dispensing with a
maidenhead
Followed by a rental car pilgrimage

To an offseason beachside cottage on Long Beach
Island
With fresh seafood, nature, protected sex and
fishing
Confirmed my new identity

We each try to shape our givens
Survive and prosper
Wish for tolerance and understanding
Be honored as parents

You were entitled to life
As were my unborn siblings
I did my best
I overcame misfortune
After my great fall
Humbled
Grateful to continue to exist
I respect creation and lineage

Peace of mind to me is
Love expressed for another being
As they love you
I forgive all
But a wall
You built
Which I can't climb

The Game to Honor

1st Place NonFiction Winner   Lena N. Gemmer

General Order 1: TO TALK TO NO ONE EXCEPT IN THE LINE OF DUTY.

We went because we were supposed to go, that's what everyone did.

Conformity breeds obedience and thus honor they said, even if we didn't agree with it... but I had some idea what they meant.

The collective "we" pulled up through the rusting gates of the *San Luis Obispo Army Base* in California, watching as the dirt from the suffocated ground whipped up a frenzy from the tires. The buildings in the distance were like the color of the sand, tan, soulless, uniform, intimidating, just like they wanted it, they wouldn't settle for anything less.

Recruit training in the summer of 2011 was a test for all of us in *The U.S. Naval Sea Cadet Core* to see if we would rank up to remain. I had originally joined up for one reason, because I wanted to play in the military band, the only one under the umbrella of this organization. But to play music, I had to first play this game. We were 14- to 17-year-old kids who had never been away from home before, except for a sleepover or two. This scene scared me... but not as much as Hawaii. Here, the orders and apparent harassment were clear and transparent. I wasn't planning on making friends.

Before we left our respective units, we were told if you were anyone, coming here in the 85-degree heat of the Central Coast Region was the right of passage to show your honor, courage, and commitment to the program, as if that was the only way. Scores of Sea Cadets came through here, first names and anything linking you to individuality always left abandoned in the car with your parents who were already questioning leaving you in such a desolate place.

I watched from the car window as every single pair of young impressionable eyes gazed up from the back seats of the rows and rows of cars at the men and women in U.S. Navy uniforms yelling at the kids who dared to get out, their dress whites flying around in the dry wind trying to escape their small adolescent shoulders.

Getting out of the vehicle, my newly fifteen-year-old self grabbed my too heavy green sea bag, suddenly second guessing signing my name away to this program. Seven months ago, when we transferred over to this organization, I had no idea what I was getting into. I was an empathetic, intuitive, and energetic kid who always had trouble fitting into molds that were not my own. Even now, looking like everyone else, I still wasn't convinced I would be accepted as a star cadet… and that intuitive kid was long gone. Ever since coming back from that band trip of a lifetime, I possessed a certain anger that I couldn't place, a certain confusion and feeling of betrayal. Whatever it was, here I was forced to put that all aside. Despite being sensitive, I had a stubborn side as well. If I left, I would be kicked out of the program and the inability to play music wasn't an option.

Within seconds, a superior officer ran up and yelled my name and a letter.

For my time here, I would be called "Seaman Recruit Gemmer, Company C," or recruit for short. I was then the lowest rank of the Sea Cadet level you could possibly go, and they made sure we knew it. Now they were going to put us through a series of tests to see if we cracked, if I cracked.

 In that moment, out of the corner of my eye I saw my parents get back in the car and drive away, realizing then all I needed to do was make it and retain my individuality, I had to win.

General Order 2. TO WALK MY POST IN A MILITARY MANNER, KEEPING ALWAYS ON THE ALERT, AND OBSERVING EVERYTHING THAT TAKES PLACE WITHIN SIGHT OR HEARING.

The next part of the game of being a Sea Cadet was stripping you down of the person you knew yourself to be. Before we knew it, we had hauled our green sea bags into the great hall, our dress whites blurring into one mass, all looking identical to each other, or so we thought.

Over on the other side of the room, rows of black stools had been placed strategically, as if someone was ready to put on a stage play, but of course, none of this happened here. We knew we were here to observe and learn.

Then four large military men stepped into the room, their eyes glancing at all of us in suspicion or casual indifference.
"Male cadets get in a line! Move!" they barked.

Quietly the males' eyes widened in confusion as they lined up by the stools, usure of what was going to happen next.

"If your home unit has not properly cut your hair to the military standards that we keep here at San Luis Obispo, then you will be getting it buzzed cut today, if you want to opt out, you can leave, but don't come back," the commander said grabbing barber tools from a blue bin.

Us female cadets were ordered to "keep seats" in formation on the cold linoleum floor, unable to leave.

A few of them snickered behind hands and chattered quietly as we watched the males sit on the stools four across, shaking like leaves.

In horror I watched as the sound of razors began to fill the room behind every male cadet. Within seconds, their hair began to fall from their ears and neck like soft feathers floating to the floor. Some cried, tears running down their cheeks, but others

just sat there frozen much like me, being forced to watch this spectacle, or stripping of individuality.
"You females stop laughing or you'll be up there next!" snarled someone behind us.

Their purpose was to teach us the first lesson for a military life- the superiors owned you. This type of humiliation was common and accepted because this is what you would get once you "joined up," after you turned 18. I knew this is what they were doing, because I had seen this type of heinous behavior before from my own superior officers in my home unit. I watched, glaring at the officers, hating the smirks on their satisfied faces.

After that event, we were instructed to our barracks for orders by the company. Walking into the room I saw hot sunlight pouring into the paned windows settling on the white walls. Rows and rows of regimented cot soldiers and wardrobes sat there waiting for us. Observing the one at the front, I realized it was curtained off from all the others. (who's is that?) I wondered, probably a superior officer.

Sitting on one of the white sheeted beds, I watched as a few girls walked over and introduced themselves with their title, last name only. Suddenly hearing dress shoes tapping on the shiny floor, we went ridged, standing beside our metal beds at attention, staring at nothing, not even the person who walked in the room.
"Welcome to San Luis Obispo, my name is Chief Kherson, you may call me Chief is that understood?!"

"Yes Chief!" We yelled in unison.

Chief Petty Officer was the highest rank you could attain in the Sea Cadets and automatically earned her respect, much unlike us. I had never seen a Chief before, and I had no idea what to expect, but after seeing how the other superiors treated the boys, I was terrified to think of how the women would treat us next. I knew too well how evil they could be.

In her dress khakis, she walked up and down to look at her new company, smirking a bit, brown eyes not matching the severity of the situation. I had no idea how old she was, but old enough to make our lives miserable If she wanted to.

She stopped right in front of me, her cropped brown hair side swept from her freckled face. I had this happen to me before, and It never ended well. Fear and anger welled up inside like a hot energy wishing I could back away, but my feet somehow refused to move.

Without saying a word, she reached over frowning, fixing my lopsided dark blue neckerchief.

I could feel my hands sweat in panic as resisted the urge to push her away, but instead, I contained myself, staring past her out the window feeling like the odd man out.
"You all look scruffy! An embarrassment to your home units! But hold no fear, I'll fix you right up. The first thing you need to learn, is to make your rack," and she began her lesson.

The more I watched her from a distance throughout the afternoon, the more I began to realize how different Chief was from all of the other superior officers I had known. She wore the Navy uniform, but also laughed at herself, talked in different voices, and danced around the barracks with glee. The Chief was only firm when she needed to be, never yelling except as a last resort. I wasn't used to this type of behavior, but I respected her for it. She at least treated us like human beings.

That night, "lights out," was at 22:00 hours, or ten o'clock. With the sun having set, there wasn't anything left they could do but let us sleep. Concealed in the moonlight in our perfectly made racks, I pulled up the scratchy green blanket up to my neck, hearing the sniffles and sobs of the girls around me, no doubt thinking of home or their pets they had just left not even a day earlier. Sadness as it happens is contagious. But I couldn't cry because if I did, I wouldn't be able to stop. Recruit training was nothing but a test that you had to beat, but at least the rules were clear. Turning over to make sure to have one eye on what was the Chief's personal barracks before falling asleep dreaming of anything other than this.

General Order 3. TO REPORT ALL VIOLATIONS OF ORDERS I AM INSTRUCTED TO ENFORCE.

"Alright recruits up up up! Three minutes to dress and get outside for PT (physical training) on the double!" and with that we were off.

The POD or plan of the day was simple and was to be followed very carefully: 0500-0600 PT, 0600-0630 chow, 0700-01100 class, and so on. There was no downtime or opportunity to think about home or the decisions that you had made in your young life to make it here, the point was to rid us of anything but the basics of military training without mistake and without complaint, so we were locked in.

I understood very quickly that everything the officers were teaching us was meant to help us become "one company," this was what they considered winning. We ate together, cleaned together, marched together. Nothing was done as an individual. If one of us messed up, then we would all be punished. This didn't surprise me all that much; I was used to it. I also knew of the mal effects it could have on someone's individuality. If you were in sync enough, your brain became a kind of "hive mind," where all the thinking was done as one unit, with no time to think about yourself. I found this to be quite ironic, since conforming seven months ago hadn't done me any favors. I was singled out anyway… would I be this time?

Later that morning, we had class that would last at least three hours. But before entering into the classroom building that looked more like an airplane shed, they distributed one small spiral bound notebook each.
 "This is your brain for the next two weeks!" Chief bellowed as we glanced at it.

Some of the kids snickered in mockery at the suggestion.

"You think this is funny, do you? Well, it's true!
You as recruits have nothing in your head, so this
notebook will help think for you! There are general
orders on the back to which you will memorize and
recite on command, am I clear?!"
"Yes Chief!" we yelled in unison.

Reluctantly, I stared at the white notebook, insulted
by its presence. I knew I already had a brain, and
there was no way they could control what I thought
about and when. Many other kids would have
conformed to whatever they wanted them to do, but
I could tell when an organization was trying to
indoctrinate me into their way of being. I began to
hate how they were treating us. This wasn't what I
signed up for, so I decided to keep fighting a little at
a time, just enough so no one would notice me not
following the rules.

All through class we were given two pencils and a
chair at a table and a reminder to never talk to one
another, or you could be kicked out. Our "brains"
began to be filled to the brim with uniform
regulations, grooming standards, naval history, and
ranking systems. At the end of each unit there was a
test, like a simulation you had to beat. At the end of
each unit, ranking systems would be put up on the
board for a healthy dose of competition. The more
my brain filled up however, the more distracted and
disgruntled I became, frustrated by the regurgitation
of information that was plaguing me, and if I
succumbed to this, they would win. Flipping in the
back of my notebook I began a secret stash, writing
little stories for myself, about a girl who was a
rebel, who defied everything and everyone and

finally escaped the fence of conformity for good. I wanted to beat this game they were playing, and the only way to do it was to break out of the mold, little by little until I too could escape.

Lena was hidden in plain sight.

Later that day we returned to the barracks to write letters home to our families. Right as we entered, I knew something was wrong. Walking into the room, I saw a woman I had never seen before. Her jet-black hair was pulled perfectly into a military bun and every crease in her Navy Working Uniform was put just right into place. The sight of her made my stomach turn. We knew then, she was going to be a hard ass, but one of the most valuable skills we learned in this environment, was how to hide and how to lie. As far as I could tell, there was no real logic to their actions. Apart from trying to make seasoned Navy cadets out of children, these officers never looked deeply into anything as long as it had the appearance of looking perfect, so that was what I decided to do, look passable. As an organization, they were so busy trying to keep order that they were unable to look past their own major flaws. All of this I understood all too well, but I couldn't worry about that just now.

Steely dark eyes scanned the room suspiciously daring us to look right at her.

"Attention recruits! Inspection will begin now! Any items that I don't find to my liking will be confiscated. You will not move or talk unless you are told to."

She started at the front room, opening the first girl's wardrobe. I could hear her pawing through clothes and drawers until she was satisfied, leaving the recruit to clean up her violation of privacy.

One by one the closer she got the more afraid I became. Even if you knew you didn't have any contraband, you were the guilty party until proven innocent. This I knew, but I was not used to having someone pawing through my things like they were a worthless extension of myself. So, at that moment, I decided to separate my mind from my personal belongings, just until she was done. If I did that, I would win this round of hazing.

Finally, in what seemed like hours, she got to me, smirking her way into my space. She wanted to make us squirm. With teeth clenched I knew every single drawer and cabinet she was opening, and what she would find.
"About face recruit!"

There was no way I was going to make her see my fear. Turning around I scowled at her, defiantly.
"What are these?" she demanded, clutching two yellow legal notepads.
"They're my notepads, just in case I needed them for class, Ma'am," I hissed locking eyes.

"Technically they are contraband, why should I let you keep them?"

I could feel every single pair of eyes in the female barracks on me as I dared to answer.
"I am a writer; writing makes my life fulfilling. I

want to keep them, they're just paper and I don't think it's harming anybody, Ma'am."

"You aren't a writer, you are a brainless recruit who should be present here and accounted for, but I'll let it slide, this time. If you are caught using them, you'll have me to answer to. You pass."

Tossing them aside, she went to her next victim, breath now able to release from my chest.

(Watch me).

General Order 11. TO BE ESPECIALLY WATCHFUL AT NIGHT, AND, DURING THE TIME FOR CHALLENGING. TO CHALLENGE ALL PERSONS ON OR NEAR MY POST AND TO ALLOW NO ONE TO PASS WITHOUT PROPER AUTHORITY.

More quickly than I learned my general orders, I learned nighttime was safe. During my first 0200 hours or 2am Firewatch, I got out of bed and grabbed my notebooks, the yellow color almost glowing neon in the moonlight rays spreading across the floor. Walking up to the recruit I was supposed to relieve, I saluted, and they handed me the log and I watched, and I waited. Firewatch was exactly what the name suggests- making sure your fellow shipmates are safe from any dangers or intruders that might dare to come by logging movements on a clipboard. Ironically, I believed the danger and intrusion were already here, within the walls. The officers, the hazing, the yelling. Looking out at my blissfully sleeping comrades I decided I was their guardian. No officer would pass by these doors without getting through Lena first to disrupt their dreams.

With that in mind, I clicked my pen, the only survival tool I had against my contraband and began to melt away into a world entirely my own, finally able to relax in my thoughts. The night was quiet, healing. Writing had always been a place I could escape to, blocking out the reality around me, absconded in my fictional protagonists who fought everything coming their way.

Here I could shed the military mask I had been holding all this time… or could I? Something had changed in me since arriving here, but I couldn't put my finger on what. It was like every day that passed, I became more and more used to the military life, and I didn't want to get used to it, because that is exactly what they wanted. Every day was a fight to sustain a piece of my individuality. It was exhausting, but I didn't want to give in. Maybe it was the organization of my wardrobe, or the way I carried myself, head held high, that made me uneasy. In some capacity I would undoubtably become *them.* The military life was rubbing off on me even if I didn't want it to. No respect had been gained from any adult here, they all had an agenda, and I could see right through it. Other cadets didn't seem to mind they were brainwashing us, giving their individuality away to the highest bidder. I had never fit in anywhere, much less here, but something told me I was beginning to just by existing in this environment.

Suddenly, I heard a bed creak. Looking up from my imagination, I saw someone from the Chief side of the room get up, her short hair a pixie silhouette in the darkness. Prior experience told me I was going to get singled out… Prior fear told me she might want something… that would include me walking over to her bed…why else would she be getting up like this in the middle of the night? There was no rhyme for this logic, no reason for me to suspect her of any maltreatment towards me…. but the last time I was around a young woman of her age in a military uniform, it hadn't ended well. In that moment, I never wished to be just like everyone else. I got up from the floor and began to look busy, checking my watch log for accuracy.

Walking under the emergency light in the doorway, she looked out at me with tired eyes. "Gemmer, what are you doing?" she groggily asked.

"Nothing Chief!" I whispered, taking a few steps back into the wall. There was something about her that told me she wasn't going to punish me…. But I still wasn't sure.

With her brown hair sticking up all over the place, she took the watch log from me. Quaking in my boots she stood in the dark silence, pursing her lips. "I saw you writing something… that wasn't this." "Yes Ma'am. I'm writing a story, I can do both watch and write." "Uh huh, let me see."

Reluctantly, I gave over my notepad, convinced I was going be kicked out…. or worse.

Looking at my writing, I saw her smile, as she often did unlike the others. Giving it back to me, Chief seemed satisfied and meandered back to bed, the night quiet again, never asking me a thing.

General Order 5. TO QUIT MY POST ONLY WHEN PROPERLY RELIEVED.

It was graduation before we knew it. July 14th, 2011, seemed to never get here fast enough for some but arrive too soon for others. Waking up that Sunday in our racks we could now make it perfectly, everything seemed to take on a new brighter shape. The end was now in sight and the end of the game was near. We girls chatted easily that day behind the barrack walls but kept a more engrained military decorum. What used to be a struggle like memorizing general orders or facts about a navy uniform was almost automatic, like nothing else was residing in our brains, just like they said. This was an undeniable fact that indeed, the training had changed in us in the way it intended to do. The reality wrangled me, for it happened so gradually, I barely knew it was happening. But there was something that they hadn't taken away from me. I sat on my rack and pulled out my notepad again, re-reading my stories that had manifested in a silent rebellion. I hadn't completely turned into these angry cruel officers, but I also embodied their teachings, so who had won the game?

Out in the open field in military formation ordered by company, with the parched grass underneath our perfectly polished shoes, the hot metal bleachers filled with smiling parents in civilian clothes holding their disposable kodak cameras for good measure. I stared straight ahead, not even wanting to look for my parents because I was convinced if they saw me, I would break the military mold and run to them wanting to jump the fence before the ceremony and I couldn't do that, still trying to settle the score within myself.

As the commanding officer stood in front of the companies, his gold banded cover glinting in the dry heat reading off the USNSCC:

"Our mission of the Sea Cadets is to build leaders of character through the core values of honor, courage, and commitment. You should be very proud of the young people behind me here folks, they are going places."

As we were dismissed, I detached myself from the symbiosis of my unit, realizing whatever had conspired throughout these last two weeks was never going away, even after stripping off my immaculate dress whites. But at the core, I realized I could remain the person I had always been, someone who knew how to fight, and eventually win, sustaining the individuality that no one could ever take away. I guess this time, I won.

A Laurel's Weight

2nd Place Fiction Winner   G. B. Croissant

The Temple of Delphi loomed in front of Mount Parnassus. Statues of Apollo and past oracles guarded the entrance, peering into my soul as I walked up the worn steps. Priestesses followed my every move, probably making sure I wouldn't run away. My stomach growled from the lack of food, and my arms stung from fierce scrubbing moments before. Nobody would want to only hear the rumblings of one's stomach instead of the glorious wisdom about to spew forth.

"Fasting is the best way to receive a prophecy," one of the older priestesses told me emphatically. I hadn't realized these meetings with Apollo would take so long to prepare for. Rituals upon rituals – a cleansing in the Castilian Spring, praying, scourging of one's body to allow the gods to see your sacrifice. Becoming the oracle was supposed to be the highest honor, a median between mortals and immortals, but the freshly made laurel crown knitting into the furrows of my brow didn't leaven the responsibility.

"You're doing fine," Panas said, touching my shoulder lightly, as if he could hear my thoughts.

I smiled weakly, holding my head up as high as I could.

The courtyard was bustling with acolytes frantically putting the last-minute arrangements of flowers and food. They all had the same nervous, scared expression. An impending doom was going to be upon us.

My eyes twinged as I watched them. My father's weakened frame hammering back and forth, dawn till after dusk, plowing fields with his sweat and blood. Mother pinning herself into whatever work she could find -- mending tunics, waiting on powerful people, making baskets to sell at open markets. Yet, bread and wine were always on the table. Their smiles haunted my dreams; even when they were on the brink of collapse, they smiled until the procession came.

Panas, less wrinkled and grey, had come with other Delphic clergymen for me.

I watched from behind our front door, unable to hear what they were saying to my parents. They had pleaded earnestly with the priests. My father shook his fists angrily, for the first time in my life.

Acolytes pushed them aside and pulled me through the door. I stood in front of Panas. I felt tears begging to flow, but I needed to be strong. I looked him straight in his eyes and pressed my lips together, determined that they wouldn't move me.

"It is the highest of honors for your family," Panas told my father. "She shall become one of the most influential people in Greece."

Drachmas were placed into father's shaking hands. He never met my eyes again as the religious parade led me away, kicking and screaming. I could hear my mother's cries as she was forced to stay behind.

I pushed the thoughts into the back of my mind.

The acolytes had arranged a chair for me to sit in on the top of the steps. I sat down with whatever dignity I had left as I watched the chaos below. A few servants tripped over each other. Someone yelled directions. A horn screamed from the distance, warning everyone as horses' hoofbeats entered our ears.

I leaned over my chair and asked Panas, "Do you know who's coming?"

"A king of some sort," he said. "The Sacred Way must've been long for him, though."

Preceding riders in elegant armor arrived and stood ready at the entrance to the pavilion. Elaborately decorated wagons pulled the last of the king's offerings to the gods – gold, silver, and animals for sacrifice. The empty carts were pulled at the back of the line. In the middle was an ornate carriage with gold-plated panels, expensive tassels, and silk draping the windows. Inside sat a man with a full beard and what appeared to be a white toga, fitted just so.

The carriage stopped at the edge of the steps and out came the king.

"King Croesus of Lydia," cried the announcer.

"That's him?" I asked. He was short and rather stubby for a king, though I had no reference for what kings should look like. His sandal-wearing feet hit the pavement with a thud.

An older priestess slapped my hand at this. "Young Pythia, control your tongue! It is not for you to judge, but the gods."

"With those looks, it should be," I muttered.

Panas stifled a laugh.

Behind the stout monarch emerged a younger, stronger version. He stood tall with an air of superiority.

"That's the prince?" I asked.

"And Prince Atys," confirmed the royal announcer.

The prince came behind his father as King Croesus bowed in my direction. The prince didn't realize until his annoyed father slapped the back of his head. The prince begrudgingly obeyed. It didn't take long for the prince to regain his regal composure from bowing to a woman. The king, satisfied, clapped his hands, which resounded to his attendants to take the appropriate offerings to the correct spots around the courtyard.

I eyed him as he padded to the edge of the steps.

"Pythia, Apollo's tongue, tell me: will I conquer Persia?" King Croesus genuflected in front of me, just a little too deeply. The son rolled his eyes. Usually, the inquirer would ask his question inside the inner sanctum, but I assessed that this king was in a hurry to get an answer, no matter the other formalities.

Some of the acolytes and priests giggled to themselves, knowing the rites better than I did. After the king asked his inappropriately spotted question, the priestesses took my arms and led me back into the inner sanctum. The king followed with his attendants. Only there would the god speak to this traveler.

The smoke from the incense burners mixed with the gases of Mount Parnassus poured into my sinuses, burning down into my lungs. My ears rang as the council prayed to Apollo for guidance. I chewed on laurel leaves, ceremoniously given to me by one of the high priests, as I waited for the god to whisper in my ears.

I could tell the king and his son grew impatient, Croesus' hair dripping from his dip in the Castilian Spring, kneeling before the altar as I tried to conjure a prophecy, allowing whatever spirit to take hold of me. I could see droplets of blood on the hem of his toga, most likely from the unfortunate goat sacrifice he made on the Sacred Path.

"Why is this taking so long?" Prince Atys exclaimed.

The priests and his father shushed him.

My eyes grew heavy from the fumes, and I felt them roll back. The burning sun blinded me. Apollo stepped into view, cradling a golden harp. I wished I could cry. His eyes were pure sunshine; his hand open and welcoming, but a looming dread crept into my heart. It seeped into my pores and flooded into my shivering hands. A maniacal grin spread over his face as a snake snuck around him, coming for me. I tried to run, but my feet were caught in the ground below.

It slithered. Closer. Closer.

The snake writhed over my taut skin, rough and burning hot. It flicked its tongue into my ear, whispering. Then, without any warning, it pried my mouth open and spilled down my throat.

My mouth opened, body spasming, and the words spilled out before I could stop them:

"King of Lydia, you ask for victory. You ask of the fates of empires."

Croesus grew silent as the voice spilled into the heavy, interested stillness.

"If you cross the Halys, a great empire will fall."

I took in a heavy, gasping breath, but the god wasn't finished.

"Seek no answers in certainty. Seek them in the turning of the wheel. The lion that leaps does not know which spear will fly. The laurel tree that

bends may yet outlive the forest. What falls may rise again."

The message resolved into a low hum in the back of my throat. As quickly as it came, it stopped. I heaved myself over my knees, palms slapping the stones beneath me.

King Croesus remained silent -- for once, since coming into the adyton -- trying to find the meaning in the words before anyone else. Priests and maidens talked in hushed tones as I regained the rest of my senses. The metal tripod cut into the backs of my trembling knees. I tried to catch my breath as my assistants ran to my side. A fan beat air against my sweat-beaded brow.

Panas touched my hands gently. "You did amazing, Pythia," he whispered. He dabbed my forehead with a small piece of cloth.

I bobbed my head solemnly.

King Croesus rose from his knees. "What does this mean?" He threw his hands down to his sides. "Tell me immediately."

Panas stepped forward. His thin white hair shone like a halo in front of the firelight. With simple words and a clear voice beyond his years, he told the king: "We do not know yet. Give us time."

"We don't have time," the prince shouted, going back to his usual tone. "If we don't make a move, Persia will surely take Lydia, and you all will be next."

"If the gods will it, then so it shall be," Panas said.

King Croesus pressed his lips together so tightly they became invisible behind his soggy beard. "How dare you speak to my son that way, priest!"

"I shall speak to those as they have spoken to me." Panas gestured for the king to kneel while they consulted among themselves. "Wait and be quiet as we work."

The king huffed as he begrudgingly kneeled again. I could see the prince's hands itching to reach for where his sword would have been. An animalistic instinct, I thought. Men were always ready to pounce on whatever they believed to be a threat, even another old man.

I regained my composure from the fumes and was led down the worn steps from the dais. I was given wine from a chalice, thinned with water.

"Was I okay?" I asked quietly.

Panas nodded. "Very well. I don't think they could tell it was your first prophecy."

The muttering priests and priestesses went on for ages. Scribes scribbled on long pieces of parchment, frantically racking their brains for the exact words that had burst uncontrolled from my mouth. I clasped my hands, nervously rubbing my thumbs across my knuckles.

~~~~~~

Everyone had left the inner sanctum long ago. The entire temple and the king's entourage had long since gone to bed, leaving me alone with my thoughts. I sat cross-legged on the cold marble floor. The air was still heavy with incense – no longer holy, but suffocating.

The god's statue loomed in front of me, towering, serene, unyielding. In the flickering of the oil lamps, Apollo's eyes almost seemed alive, fixed on my movements.
~~~~~~

I clasped my hands together. "Lord Apollo, why do you make me speak what I don't understand?"

My words dissolved in the silence. The statue stared at me with the same blank gaze, as if it would change with my words.

"Do you delight in my confusion?" I tried again, louder this time. "How do I honor you if I let people walk willingly into their ruin? Is this what you demand of me?"

The unanswered questions echoed against the stone walls.

I replayed how King Croesus had come into the courtyard, determined and proud. He seemed to believe himself chosen for greatness, though my lips trembled with the truth he was unable to see.

If you cross the Halys, a great empire will fall.

How easy was it for him to hear victory? How easy was it to keep a closed mouth and let the phrases live on?

I pressed my forehead into the floor. "I am your mouth, not your conscience," I repeated to myself, trying to will it into truth. "I am yours. I am yours. I am--"

After a few minutes, they no longer made sense. It felt like chains. Was this the honor of being an oracle? To be a hollow vessel without a will? I sat back on my heels. Practicing the flow of prophecies led others to ruin. Those before me became the essence of harm, or the ambiguity of what was to come. Never straightforward. How could this bring any good?

"I wish I could speak as myself."

A faint sound of soft footsteps stirred behind her. I turned to see an elder priest watching from the doorway. His gray hair was sticking out at all angles, as if he had rolled out of his cot to be here. His clothes hung around his lanky body, bones jutting out from his paper-thin skin.

"You pray too loudly, child," he said. "Do you wish to wake everyone?"

"I'm sorry, Panas," I replied. "I was just thinking out loud."

Panas nodded and sat down next to me. "There are many things we don't understand. And it's not our job to do so. Our god is many things, but being clear about our fate isn't one of them. We listen, obey, and honor what we think is right."

"What if what we think is right is wrong?"

"Then we must trust in ourselves and that the gods have put those thoughts in our heads for a reason. But, as a vessel of Apollo, you aren't allowed the same liberties as the rest of us," he warned. His lined face was stern in the lamplight. "You must bear whatever your worries are and give them up to the gods."

"What does that mean?"

He patted my knee. "Pray on it. Quietly."

Panas stood on trembling knees, stretching the creaks out of his back.

I sat there for a long time, watching the eyes of Apollo follow my movements. My hands began to go numb from rubbing them together in frustration. There wasn't anything I could do. Every day since I had been chosen, they all said to trust in him and be his tongue. An empty vessel. But what if I could save an entire country? I could help. The prophecy was vague enough to be interpreted both ways, but I could tell by how much the king had wanted to be about the Persians, my gut felt the opposite. Lydia would fall.

When the sun began to rise over the great Mount Parnassus, staining the sky with brilliant purples and oranges that spread throughout the small wisps of clouds, I stopped by the thin stream that ran between the mountain and the grove next to the temple—a moment of peace. Dipping my hands into the water, I rinsed the loose laurel leaves from my hair.

A soft thudding of feet on the ground made me turn to the side, expecting an acolyte to have found me.

"My king," I said, bowing low. "You should not be here."

King Croesus waved his hand. "No king comes here. Only a man in need of a conversation with a woman connected to the gods."

I furrowed my eyebrows, growing suspicious. "Lord, I do not think this is appropriate. I may be the god's tongue, but I am not here to give advice other than that."

The Lydian king stepped forward with slow, deliberate movements. "It isn't the god I fear. It is men. Persians. You told me that if I crossed the Halys, a great empire would fall. My generals believe that the empire means Persia." He paused. "But I am no fool to these prophecies. I have heard tales of Apollo's words – how often they can cut both ways. Tell me the truth. Is it my empire that will burn?"

My throat tightened. I knew the rules, branded into my memory: I was not allowed to speak outside the inner sanctum of the mount—no offering of comfort, warning, or any personal interpretation.

"I cannot --"

"You cannot – or will not?" He stepped even closer. "I am not blind, Pythia. You know more than you said in that room. You saw something in the smoke that you won't tell anyone. Tell me."

I clenched my fists at my sides. "The god's words are his alone. I cannot alter them in any way, or I would defy him."

"Yet you are flesh and blood. The same as me." His face softened. "Do you think I came here searching for definitive glory? The great Alexander, who came before, chasing endless conquests, is not my inspiration. I came here in search of a path for my people's future. My son's future."

"Your son?" The wrathful brute of a boy didn't need saving from others. Himself, perhaps.

Croesus laughed bitterly. "Well--" He took a deep breath. "I will have to send away. Marry him off to keep the bloodline going, and all that. If Lydia falls, I need to ensure my boy is safe. Gods forbid that my line ends with me, even if my crown is ground into dust."

My breath caught in my chest slightly. This wasn't the boastful, impatient king from the ceremony and the courtyard. This was a man hoping for survival, not for himself, but for those he loved.

"You would exile your son?" I said quietly.

"I would do anything to save him." His eyes met mine – watering and desperate. "Tell me, young Pythia, am I sending him to safety or his doom?"

Apollo's oath clanged around in my head. "I-I..."

"I am a king. You must obey me!"

I turned around. My insides churned. If I disobeyed the gods and someone found out, I would be exiled. I would be thrown out of the order and shamed. But something gnawed at me. I could help.

"Do not cross the Halys," I said. "Persia will not be destroyed. I fear Apollo is warning you to leave the border where it is or Lydia will fall."

The words hung in between us like a knell.

Croesus closed his eyes, jaw tightening. "That's what I feared."

Air lodged itself in my chest, constricting my heart. What had I done? I couldn't take the words back – back to the safety of great Apollo's ambiguity – but these could not be unsaid.

Croesus, after a few seconds, nodded, as if sealing some unspoken vow to himself. "Then I will go all the same. But my son shall be sent to Sardis when the time comes. I thank you, Pythia... not Apollo, you."

King Croesus of Lydia turned around, his toga swirling around him in a flurry of dirty white. His guards, who had been standing quietly at the edge of the clearing, escorted their king away into the surrounding dusk.

I sank to my knees by the trickling stream, hand and lips trembling. The laurel crown slid from my head, landing on the stones beside me. One of the leaves had turned brown and curled in the growing light.

Prince Atys burst through the doors, his armed guards in tow. He pointed a finger at me, his other hand clutching a sword so tightly his knuckles were white from strain.

"Pythia, mistress of Apollo," he rumbled, "you killed my son."

I stared at him, head tilted, studying him as his guards surrounded the altar. I was between the intruders and the back of the mountain, once again seated on the tripod. Advisors stood as a barrier between me and the supposed threat.

"You do this, and Apollo will rain holy terror on you, Croesus," warned Panas. Though his frail hands held years of experience, they didn't waver, holding them up in supplication.

Panas gripped my shoulder. "What did you do?"

"She lied to me!" he spat. "You said we would win. We would all live."

Panas turned to me, his eyes seething with disappointment.

I stood tentatively on the top of the altar. "My prince--"

"I am a king! Yet my throne is nothing but ashes. Cyrus claimed the entire country. My father--" His voice broke. He regained his composure within seconds, hardening. "You said we would win if my father went to war. A great empire would fall."

My heart thudded against my ribs.

"And so the prophecy foretold," Panas interjected. He glanced between both of us.

"Not Perisa!" He laughed bitterly. "The young Pythia told King Croesus plainly that he would win. He was supposed to be victorious, and I, his son, would be safe if I were sent away. Tell me, Oracle, was this your god's cruelty or your own?"

I did this. I let an empire fall unnecessarily. Lives lost because he didn't listen.

"You were warned not to cross the Halys," Panas said. "The oracle has nothing to do with your foolish actions."

"You blame me for this false prophecy? She said this to the king directly." Prince Atys waved his sword, pacing in aggravation. "No, this was outside the temple, the morning after the prophecy. She promised my father Apollo would be on our side, victorious."

I felt myself intuitively shrink back onto the stool. Panas was expressionless, motionless. Then he slowly started backing away from his place at my side. I had used my voice instead of Apollo's.

"I did what I thought was right," I whispered.

Atys paused his heavy steps. "You ruined me! My father is gone!"

"Would you rather I stay silent while you marched? I told him what I knew to be right. Even so, he didn't heed my warning and failed to keep Lydia."

"You are his voice," he scoffed. "Now all I see is a weak, scared girl."

My eyes stung. Panas stepped between the king and the altar stairs, pleading hands up. "We shall get this sorted out."

Atys pursed his lips. "This witch should be burned for her insolence."

"I assure you, there will be punishments."

"Live with the knowledge that you destroyed thousands of lives with your words, Pythia." He pointed his sword at me again. "Live and suffer."

With the few guards he arrived with, they flew
back out of the Temple of Delphi.

All eyes were on me as the tears streamed down
my face, knowing my fate was sealed.

~~~~~~

Panas and the other clergy sat on stone blocks
placed around the courtyard. A blessed fire was lit
in the middle of the circle. I kneeled with the fire to
my back, awaiting my final judgment. My laurels
sat in front of me, a burden waiting for restoration.

"Appointed Pythia of Apollo, Mistress of
Prophecy and Median to the gods," said Panas,
being head of the presidial council. "You have been
accused of giving false prophecies to your inquirers.
State your case."

My teeth pressed together to keep the tremor
from my voice. The mountain air filled my lungs,
and in my mind, I felt Apollo's serpent coil close,
steadying my heart.

"I was not wrong," I started. "Nor was I right in
what I did. What I told King Croesus was sound.
My words were a warning-- to him, not his enemy."

The priests and priestesses murmured between
themselves, but I pressed on.

"I erred in speaking to him outside the sanctum,
without witnesses. I know that. But he came to me
in confidence."

"The rules are plain," an older priestess said
sharply. "You know them by heart."

"I do," I agreed. "And among them is this: I am
a servant to the people, not only a mouthpiece for
Apollo. Do I not have a duty to honor those who
come to me with questions? None of you can
~~~~~~

intercede with the gods like I can. I did what was expected of me."

Panas watched me intently, pressing his first fingers together up to his chin. His brow was tight with thought, sweat tracing the deep trenches. Friend or not, he was my judge today.

"Call me a liar or a deceiver," I said. "But what I told King Croesus came to pass."

The counsel, once bubbling with chatter, now sat steeped in deep thought, each member wrestling with their ethical convictions.

The elder priestess, who had spoken earlier, stood. "You gave him truth. He chose his path. This is the way of the Oracle -- to be a mouthpiece, yes, but also the ear of men. And ears often hear what they want."

The elders conferred in low tones. The fire crackled with anticipation, its heat pressing into my shoulder blades. After a few minutes of heated arguments among the elders, Panas held up his hands for quiet.

"We are the keepers of god's word," he said. If we weigh it with the happiness of men, we fail our charge." He came forward. "Let us go and reflect upon our revelations. Quietly."

My old friend picked up my laurel wreath and placed it back on my head. The weight was familiar now -- and heavier.

June New Moon Special

Betrayers Whisper Far Too Loud

Rowan Quinn

Deep where silence breeds,
A throne of bones and broken deeds,

A crown of scars upon the brow,
Bears weight of sins no one speaks of now,

With loyalty worn like a shroud,
Betrayers whisper far too loud,

The sacred code, once pure and bright,
Dissolves in darkness, out of sight.

What virtue dwells in hollow eyes,
When masks conceal the truth and lies?

Beneath the surface, secrets rot,
A festering wound, a silent knot,

For what is valor, if not a guise,
A mask that hides the truth's demise?

The Piss Poor Martyr, The Bus Stop Hound

Jacob Williams

Who gave you that bruise? The one around your eye, the color of bruised cabbage. The shape of it too. Does it hurt to blink, still? Did you give as good as you got? Who taught you how to cover your face, just high enough, like this? Dixon Shelby's father Bill used to call it a "pop quiz" when he would teach his son how to put a guard up, a good one. He'd keep peppering Dixon's chin with soft punches and no warning. Bill would only stop when he could tell his son was punching back harder than the last time. This is what Bill believed, as a father. The truth. He never lied to his son about anything. He tried to share every lesson he had ever learned. Even if Bill didn't remember who with, or why, he made sure Dixon heard every story of every fight Bill had ever won. "A lifetime of a bloody education," he said. And a two way deal. Even now at age thirty, Dixon still trades stories with his dad, like football practice, like a Sunday meal. Fight stories were a can't miss tradition for them, for decades, a rope that tied together their lives.

Until three years ago, when Dixon called Bill from a gravel parking lot, to tell his dad one more fight story. Actually, Dixon's only honest fight story. While picking rocks from his pants and tasting blood from rattled teeth, he confessed to so many different lies. Now, Dixon, living only a few

minutes from home, coaching football again,
teaching history, and sometimes still joining his dad
in a deer blind remembers that morning through the
quiet. The absolute silence on the other end of the
phone as he admitted that this was his first fight
ever, not just his first loss. Dixon had told his dad a
dozen stories before: brawls in locker rooms,
shoving matches at house parties. "Every single
one…bullshit…" Dixon said. He had been lying to
his dad for as good as forever. Now, whenever the
two are walking through the woods, or sitting at a
diner near dawn, Dixon can remember that morning
through how empty it was, how much his dad was
"just fucking listening." Dixon didn't know what
more to say.

Bill wasn't normally the "listening" kind of guy.
Hell, Bill once chased a referee to his car,
screaming about a foul against nine-year-old Dixon
in a football game. It was for dancing after a sack.
Something Bill always told his son to do. He said,
"If you aren't gonna spend the whole paycheck,
why even work to pay day?" The referee disagreed.
Bill refused to accept that. He didn't care that
Dixon's team had won anyway. He didn't care that
Dixon wasn't crying anymore. Nobody went with
Bill as the referee drove away and then he did too.
Bill never told anybody what happened next.
Neither did Dixon's mom Sandra, or anybody else
Bill might have told back then. The last thing Dixon
remembers is how red his dad's face was. How
much Bill's entire body was shaking. Like either
Bill was going to explode, or everybody else would
around him.

Which is exactly what Dixon imagined, again, all those years later. Across the phone, he could hear how hard Bill was grinding his teeth, in order to not "drive across the state and beat your ass." Dixon understood. This wasn't just a lie. This was a long knotted noose of them stretching back their entire lives. A rotted foundation to everything they knew about each other. The one lie Dixon never planned on confessing to anyone. Until that bloody morning, when across the parking lot, after their fight, a little boy in football pads was trying to help the other guy walk away with dignity. Dixon watched them while he picked himself up off the ground, alone. It was like he had finally figured out something he never understood, watching that. Something he needed Bill to hear. As long as his dad would "just fucking listen."

Dixon had spent his entire life listening to his dad, even if he didn't always understand what was being said. If he felt a few steps behind his dad. Behind what made Bill so confident, loud, entrenched in his beliefs. Dixon believed, if his dad had been a preacher, Bill would have been an old testament kind of guy—eye for an eye, hellfire and brimstone, never look back or get blessed into motherfucking salt. Dedication and anger side by side with no borderlines. A lifetime before he was a dad, Bill was raised the middle boy of seven brothers, in a small town somewhere south of St. Louis. Dixon has never been told where or taken to visit, but Bill always said it was the kind of place where if anybody you knew got into trouble, you always did too. That was how everybody survived, he said. If one of Bill's brothers kissed the wrong girl and got jumped at the back of the school bus, Bill was climbing over the seats with his fists already bound. If Bill threw a rock in the wrong car window, their whole house would empty out until the neighborhood was quiet again. And if anybody saw Bill alone on the street and started charging him, he didn't need to care why, he just needed to defend himself and whoever he was fighting for. Loyalty wasn't the name of the game, but it was always how you kept playing. And if he didn't fight back, Bill knew, he wouldn't always have the luxury of raising his fists. He was going to have to "fight somebody, somewhere, by the end of any day," so he might as well get it out of the way when he could.

This is not the world Dixon was raised in, even if it was always right next door, waiting at the corner of his eyes, chasing him down over the years. The boogeyman in Dixon's closet. Something that didn't matter when he was with his dad because his dad never lost. But as soon as Dixon got dropped off at school or at his mom's, it was like everything changed. Everything he believed in turned from iron to glass in his hands. He lost a grip on something necessary. And no matter what his mom, or teachers, coaches said, without his dad, that was always how he felt. Even as an adult coaching football, Dixon would ask himself what Bill would do, if he were here. Even if he was never going to agree. It was a handful of stars up in the night, to run by.

But when those stars were gone half the time, Dixon was wandering in an absolute dark.

Stumbling over himself. Alone. Dixon's mom, Sandra never understood Bill, but she thought she knew her son enough, naturally. So for his sixth birthday, she bought him an old school composition notebook, black and white. Dixon's parents had gotten divorced earlier that year and his mom started sitting down with him every night to write. Whenever she got home from teaching, she would make both of them dinner. Then before Dixon could do anything else, she would put the notebook down on the table. She never had the energy to tell one more kid what to write, but she always said he couldn't get dessert or leave the kitchen until he wrote something down. Even before he could face all of his letters the same way, she just told him to cover every page. Easy enough. He took to the writing like a chore that first year, but by the time he was in the fourth grade, even when his mom forgot, Dixon couldn't go to bed without picking up a pencil and a notebook. It became an instinct. The same as his breathing or the way he caught a football. So easy, he didn't even think about what he wrote down. Dixon didn't notice that he wrote down different things after days with his mom versus dad . He didn't realize that even when he had heard the same stories, he was still memorizing them, because the details were always different. Details he could carry in his hand this way. Details he could always turn into something else, later on.

In all fairness, Dixon did think to call his mom first, the morning of that fight. Before it was even over, he knew he would need help. He had never been fired before. Or, god forbid, gotten arrested. But he also knew she wouldn't really be able to listen, right now. Would she hear his split lip over the phone? Would she call the cops herself?. Would she understand if he had to hang up because the fight wasn't over? For better or for worse, all of the shit that had just hit Dixon's fan was Bill's shit. Dixon was a creature they both had built, but right now it was his dad's hands at his side, his dad's blood in his veins. It was long past time, he realized that he leaned back on those reflexes. That he started trying to remember why he wrote down any of those stories in the first place. The way his mom taught him to. Even if that wasn't what Bill would have said. Dixon would always have to do both, somehow. That was his family. His only family.

Yes, Bill had over a half dozen brothers, and more cousins than he ever sat down to count, but he never told his dad or brothers about Sandra and Dixon. As far as anyone else knew, Bill hadn't talked to anyone back home since he left for the army. In Bill's opinion to this day, family is only as important as what a person can do with their own two hands. What someone can build for their family. That was the point of every splinter of Bill's life. What good are laws, hospitals, governments stacked so far above your head to bruise the clouds, when one lucky punch could come at any moment? What was standing there between your face the way it is now and afterwards? All questions of fairness and pride were immediately settled when Bill would pull the front two teeth dripping from his gums, and talk about the beatings he had seen a kid take, just because they weren't looking when the first guy swung, or when the ball was hiked.

Bill played football his entire life, until he went into the army. When he got back from Vietnam, he had a tattoo of a little football on his biceps, with the year he had graduated and won the state championship right in the middle. Dixon played even longer, through college, sometimes with Bill as a coach, and sometimes not. He only ever scored a touchdown though, once, in high school. He was playing offensive lineman and just happened to be in the right place at the right time to scoop a fumble and fall across the endzone. He was jogging back to the sidelines, listening to the crowd and still holding the ball when he caught Bill yelling from behind the bench. As soon as Dixon was close enough, Bill yanked his son's wrists off the field and knocked the ball to the ground. He held his son's hands like if he let go he would lose them. Even as Dixon got pulled back by his teammates, Bill kept holding, just as tight. He couldn't look away from his teenager's fingers, like he had carved every curve and every crack himself. Bill was always proud of his son, he said, no matter what. That was his job as Dixon's father. "The work of my lifetime…" Bill said. But he also told Dixon, "…the work ain't ever done…breaks are for the finished"

After that first touchdown, the next morning they were still out in the woods before sunrise. Every other Saturday, they were out in the same trees, in the dark. Until Dixon was 18, this was the other half of life. Fighting and football were how you defended yourself in the middle of everyone. Hunting and hiking were for the middle of nowhere. Once you were hopeless, alone. Dixon was past the age at this point of being carried, but he still barely remembers anything before they got up in that tree. Then, as his luck held up, he bagged his first buck that morning." This is your weekend, champ!" Bill cheered after Dixon caught it cleanly right behind the front legs after only an hour of his dad's whispering filled up the dawn. Both of them were hooting and hollering before they could even get down on the ground but only Dixon got quiet as they walked towards the body. It was silly, stupid he knew, but Dixon had never seen anything dead before. Never even imagined it. Until he was "lucky."

Bill and Dixon had never talked about why they were out there. The first few years, Bill would just carry his son and a tinfoil breakfast sandwich out to the car, without words. Then in the years after that, it just became another habit. The way most of his weekends with his dad went b. Muscle memory. As long as Dixon did what his dad told him to and did it often enough, he could pass the time somewhere else in his head. That morning though, he knew he'd never forget the weight of that deer's body. Or his dad's words as Bill explained, standing over the dead thing, what Dixon was going to have to do with every deer bagged, from here on out. At least, as long as they were using Bill's stand, his guns, and his ammo. Dixon would have to carry every kill either of them made back to the car, on his own and after he learned how to, he was going to have to field dress it, on his own, every time. It wasn't just "a fair shake", Bill said, it was also "the price of admission to the game."

A game, Dixon would never play alone, even if
his dad didn't always help. Dixon could never
doubt his dad on that. If Bill was anything
alongside loud, generous, and heavy-handed, he
was there. Whether it was over meals, sports, or
homework. When Bill got a call from his son in the
middle of the night, he always answered, and Bill
never hung up until Dixon was fast asleep on the
other end of the line. Sometimes Bill'd still just sit
there and listen to the quiet. Not a moment was still
or wasted. Dixon learned how to stay clear of
poison ivy on those walks. How to pump his arms
with his legs before practice. How to memorize his
multiplication tables with riddles and rhymes. Bill
was constantly practicing his math while driving
from jobsite to jobsite. At a certain age, Dixon
might have tried to run from this trait of his dads,
shake off that constant presence like a mosquito.
But when he was young, he questioned his dad like
the sunshine, like the breeze. He didn't know how.
Dixon could rely on Bill, always, like that.

Always, that is, except for Sunday. That was
another rule Dixon was raised on. Another thing he
was never taught to question. Every Sunday was the
only day that Bill could not be reached, could not
be bothered. From the time that Dixon could wipe
his own butt to once his time with his dad was
always scheduled in advance. Why? Because
Sundays were Bill's cleaning days. His own
unshakeable version of the holy day. As soon as the
sun was up on Sunday morning, whatever tv Bill
had access to would be in the center of his house
waiting for the first kickoff, as he gathered all of the
sprays, sponges, and buckets hidden away. The day

then wouldn't end until every surface had been scrubbed, every stone turned over, on his hands and knees for as long as it took. No matter who he had to ignore, scream with, or walk past, Sundays were a day just for Bill. They were also the only day's Dixon ever actually saw his parents fight. And the only days Dixon's dad ever yelled at him.

When Dixon called his dad, that morning, it was Saturday. But Sunday would be the day his dad drove up to help him pack the little apartment a few blocks from the school. As well as the classroom Dixon would no longer be able to teach in. The job he knew he was going to lose, because of the parent he got into a fight with. Bill never mentioned that it was Sunday. Honestly, Dixon didn't notice, until he was telling his mom the whole story later. Just as he spent that whole day telling his dad the story of the fight. His dad would ask for it again and again. Like it had happened years ago. And every time Dixon told it, his dad would have another question. Another detail he had missed or already forgotten. Another part that he didn't understand. Dixon has told his dad his only fight story now easily a hundred times, in only the past three years, always trying to keep his details the same. Just trying to help his dad find whatever the two of them are looking for, together. Leading a horse to some water, so that both of them can drink.

It was twenty years before the weekend of the fight, that Bill had chased the referee down the interstate, but not much had changed. Bill was never going to be the best listener. Dixon's parents still don't talk. But neither of them has remarried, either. Dixon has always tried to figure that out, too. There was one night in spring, when Dixon was in high school, and he was watching his mom struggle the worst he ever saw. She had just gotten laid off, after finding out that a cousin of hers had died in California. There was no way she could afford the plane ticket anymore, but she went anyway and called Dixon every night, asking if the lights were still on and the house was still standing. Dixon was sixteen and he said everything he could. Then when that wasn't enough, he would just listen and write down what she was saying in his notebooks. The fears she had for them both, the regrets she normally wouldn't show anyone, let alone her son. Then the third day that she was gone, Bill showed up at the house with his truck full of cleaning supplies. Dixon didn't know how Bill knew. He didn't know Bill still had a spare key. Bill didn't explain anything.

Dixon skipped school that Monday to clean his mother's house, with his dad. They moved every piece of furniture out into the yard, scrubbed every ceiling and every wall. Dixon didn't ask any questions or complain but he couldn't move his arms much by the time the sun went down, when his dad then washed every piece of clothing in the house, washing by hand what he couldn't get into each consecutive washer load. At the end of the day, like the past few days, Dixon's mom called him and he didn't think to lie or keep any secrets. He was surprised when his mom didn't know Bill was there. She asked Dixon why he had let his dad inside the house without asking her first. She told Dixon to make his dad leave, right away, and Dixon

told her that he would. She made him promise.
Then Bill didn't notice when Dixon stopped
helping, even after he ordered a pizza for them and
just sat in the kitchen, describing his dad's work in
his notebooks and quietly eating. Bill never asked
for any more help. Dixon still thinks about that day,
as he cleans every Sunday now in his own house.
He remembers watching his dad like a machine that
somebody forgot to turn off. That night, Dixon fell
asleep to his dad still working, like distant thunder,
and woke up to the front door locked and a text on
his phone saying where to find the spare key. Bill
said he would see Dixon at his next football game,
in a handful of days.

Dixon never understood his dad less than
when he did stuff like that. When he dove headfirst
into murky waters, guaranteed, to break his head
open on a rock just as likely as he might save
somebody's life. Bill was a piss-poor martyr, Dixon
thought, trying to somehow force a sacrifice, break
a miracle with the weight of his body against life,
like a hole in a wall. Meanwhile, Dixon would be
sitting at the edge of the beach, praying nobody
needed an ambulance and feeling just as much as
his dad, watching the ripples and getting only his
feet wet.

Not to say that Dixon grew up a lonely boy. He
was shy and a little awkward, but by the time his
dad was married twice and raising his only kid,
Dixon could name half a dozen adopted uncles from
his dad's work at construction sites or his nights at
various dive bars, as well as their own kids and
spouses. Most weekends that Bill had his son were

colored with late night watch parties for any championship fight or bowl game, where Bill's house would be filled no matter where he was living. His dad always had friends, Dixon could say. Which is also the only reason Dixon ever doubted his dad, back then. One night, the summer that Dixon turned thirteen, he was brought outside by Bill holding a pair of torn, stiff boxing gloves, and the announcement that Dixon was about to prove himself. There was going to be a fight.

"Wait, the fight on TV?" Dixon asked.

"In the living room," Bill said, "Our own undercard match. Terry thinks just cuz his boy turned thirteen first, y'all are equals. If that little runts got a snowball's chance in hell-"

"I don't…what do you mean? I don't want to fight anybody."

"Remember what I've told you about the family jewels, forget that for one night and one night only. Terry Junior may be in the way, but his dad's still a buddy. Keep it clean? This ain't really fighting, just a little bit of fun, ya hear me?"

Then, Bill went back inside, leaving Dixon alone with the gloves on, to practice, and to look across the front yard of his dad's place, into the summer darkness like a luxury, like snowfall in the woods. Dixon couldn't see much down the road, but he could remember where the neighborhood opened up. His mom didn't live that far away, without any highways in the middle. Dixon would recognize which grocery store to go past, the restaurant to turn at, the water tower that sat at the back of her street. Without a buck of any size on his back, it would be easy, he thought.

When Bill came back, Dixon didn't ask how much money was on the line, if he could drink his first beer before the insanity, or if this was all really about to happen. Behind his dad's back, he could see a kid that was practically his cousin already holding some gloves tightly to his own cheeks. Just the way Bill always said to. Just the way Dixon was taught.

There wasn't going to be a fight that night, Dixon knew right then. Not one that he was in, at least. Dixon wasn't sure how he knew, but it was like he just decided it, that night. No matter what his dad said, or did, he thought about how easy it would be for Bill to go back inside alone and make up some lie. He tried to guess how much more he might have to run at the next practice his dad brought him to, or the next time they were out in the woods. But Dixon also knew, those things were going to happen anyway, the older he got. Whether it was one fight, or a hundred, Dixon realized his dad wouldn't change.

Bill was the dog that waited at the bus stop. The old barking thing that never moved for anybody else, no matter how much food, shelter, or noise they threw his way. In the rain, heat, or snow, he'd be found by the roadside, until the person he was waiting for came back to town. If they ever did at all. And that person wasn't always Dixon, but on that night, there was nothing he could do that his dad wouldn't sit through, wouldn't watch, wait, and listen to. He could feel it. So he wasn't going to fight.

Less than an hour later, Dixon watched from the kitchen table, the same place he would get help with algebra homework come Monday night, as another boy wore his father's gloves, and as Terry Junior swung wildly, smashed a punt sized hole in a living room window and upset somebody's dog with his screaming. The chihuahua grabbed onto TJ's leg and wouldn't let go of the meat for anyone. By the time the window was covered in cardboard from somebody's truck, the dog was calmed down, the leg was wrapped up and bandaged, and the dad's decided what to do with the money that was bet, the main event match on tv was over already. Everybody had missed the actual fight.

Dixon remembers that night, thinking he had it all figured out. Like the next time Bill was driving him to football practice, he could just as easily wrench the steering wheel from his dad's hands, send the car into a ditch, change everything. Like he hadn't already done that, every day of his life. Dixon loved football. He always would. He missed those long hikes in the trees, after he moved away for college. He loved his dad. More than he would have, maybe, if they weren't together so much. Bill wouldn't have been the same man. And of course, this isn't how Bill would have talked about himself. Not to this day, what he would ever call any of it. Bill has never once used the phrase, "fight stories." Dixon doesn't really either. Even the most violent or repeated tales are just the memories Bill can't help but share. He has football stories too, and work stories. Stories of Dixon as a baby that he's told after just as many beers. Like the time Dixon pooped his diaper so much in Sandra's arms, it went up the infant's back and covered his own hair like a helmet. Dixon could have just as likely filled notebooks with any of those. He could have lost everything he had now, just like that.

It was only a few months before his first fight that Dixon started coaching football. He stayed in the same city he went to college in. He never planned on moving back home. He didn't plan on coaching either. When he graduated, after starting as a lineman for two years, he just wanted to teach. Honestly, he didn't know what he wanted, but with a degree in education and knees that couldn't even joke about trying for professional ball, he landed where he could. He taught seventh graders about the American revolution for a year, went and supported the students that played for the team, even talked to them about the plays they were learning. Then when one of their dads had to start working nights, one of the kids asked Dixon for his help. It was just the C-team, he told himself. It was just for a year.

When he eventually called Bill to share the news, Dixon had to pull the phone away from his ear. He hadn't heard Bill string together so many celebratory curse words since he was in high school. It gave Dixon an excuse to call his dad every Saturday again, too, after college gave him an excuse to pretend he didn't care. He was honest with himself about that. After every game, once the field was cleaned off and the coach's office locked up, Dixon would carry his duffel to his car and call his dad on his way to breakfast. He could imagine Bill sitting next to him, even if he never thought about why that mattered. Even if he never told Bill the reason for the calls. Sometimes they'd just go over the next holiday Dixon would be heading home. Sometimes they'd go over the day's football game play by described play. Sometimes, Dixon would ask his dad for help.

Especially in the beginning, when he found himself diving headfirst into so many kid's lives. Differently than in the classroom, he felt. Coaching football felt like, "putting a handgun in twenty different puppies' mouths, waiting for somebody's tongue to find the trigger." Bill laughed his ass off at that one. Told Dixon to, "trade those pistols for a box of hand grenades and get those dogs a championship!" Dixon faked a laugh whenever his dad gave advice like that. He tried to find what he was looking for in the words. He didn't know what he was doing. He couldn't stand it when a player of his got hurt. Especially when it happened outside of practice or a game. Dixon couldn't help but see himself in the kids running before and after everything, with a dad in the bleachers chewing on a whistle he brought from home.

That was the dad that broke a few of Dixon's teeth, eventually. Another dad that Dixon had lied to. He had said the guy's kid couldn't start that morning. He had said the kid just wasn't good enough anymore. Which couldn't hold a drop of water. Everyone knew that boy was the best linebacker Dixon had. Even kids off the team called him Moose. Dixon didn't care. He stopped caring when he saw the kid limping in the hallways one week. He knew he could have had a better lie, but it was too late. It didn't matter anymore, when he heard the crunching footsteps behind him. When he turned to see the bearded semi-truck of a man already at his chest, grabbing Dixon by the shoulders, falling with him to the ground. Dixon was just squinting his eyes against the sunlight, when the first punch fell. Knuckles that threw his whole head towards the right. Sent his jaw farther it was meant to go. He could feel it.A dozen different things breaking at once, as every bone and muscle in his head reacted. Like a whole team moving when the ball gets thrown. Violence orchestrated. Nothing else attached. Everything was so far away.

"Pa, I said stop!"

Dixon tried to look up at the source of that voice, when another fist came straight at his lips. That's when the blood started pouring. Not from his forehead, or his nose, like on TV with the guys in the cage. Dixon tasted it before he knew what it was. He felt pieces in his mouth with his tongue that he couldn't make sense of. Angles that hadn't existed before. A wall broken into bricks. Another fist came down, but this time Dixon got his guard up, got his own hands in the way, his forearms taking the brunt of the damage. Bruises left with every knuckle. A consolation prize. Muscle memory.

So this is what it was like. The other side of so many of Bill's stories. Dixon couldn't remember how much his dad ever described the other guy. At a certain point, it would just be sadistic. Maybe the guy holding Dixon down was sadistic. The guy holding him down? Dixon didn't realize he was laying on his own until his eyes adjusted a little bit more. Until he started breathing through the blood in his mouth.

"What do you think I meant, by stay in the car?" That was the voice of the semi-truck. The man that Dixon could only describe from a distance or way too up close. He didn't know the guy's name.

Nobody else said anything and Dixon forced himself to sit up. The guy was standing a dozen yards away, his back to Dixon. Breaking one of Bill's rules. The guy was looking down at his son. The two were just staring at each other. Moose looked so much smaller standing next to his dad, instead of the rest of the football team. Dixon couldn't remember the kids name either, as he climbed back to his feet. As he spat something out on the ground. Might have been a piece of a tooth, or just a glob of blood. When it landed, both of them looked over at Dixon, like he had caught them in something. Dixon was holding a rock. Like he wasn't the one who put it there.

Moose was holding onto his dad's arm when the guy turned back to face Dixon. Moose didn't let go. The guy turned as much as he could, to stare Dixon down. To notice the rock.

"Dad?" Moose was pulling on the guy now. With all of his weight, trying to rip both of them out of this moment. Throw them anywhere else. It wasn't working.

"Go back to the car." Dixon said then, or at least tried to. He could hear his own voice in his head, and also he could hear the grumble of shattered letters coming out of his mouth.

"Don't you fucking talk to my kid, don't you talk to him ever!" Moose's dad then turned his back to Dixon again, strike two, and got down on his knees, to look at Moose. He put a red-knuckled hand on his son's shoulder and said some words Dixon couldn't fully hear across the distance. They weren't for Dixon. "...trust me, just go…call when it's…ya hear me…"

Dixon dropped the rock, as he stood there. He didn't want to kill anyone. Even if that wasn't how his dad would have done this. Bill wasn't there.

Bill wasn't there, Dixon watched the guy hug his son and then let go. As he realized, the fight wasn't over. Maybe it had barely even started. Even without Bill here, Dixon was still doing this. No matter how little he wanted to. Who was he trying to impress? Who could he blame? Would it always be like this?

Dixon was running, before the other guy could turn around, before Moose could really get away from them. He was running before he knew why. This was a gift, wasn't it? All of the instincts, and the knowledge. The goddamned muscle memory from lifetimes that weren't his. Even if it was never wanted, was a gift always a gift? You weren't supposed to ask for it, right? Moose hadn't asked for this. As Dixon caught his dad off guard and tried to kick the "family jewels" clean in half.

Dixon watched Moose fall too, jumping to his dad's side. The toughest kid on the field, with real skills, an understanding. "You aren't ever fighting, if you aren't fighting dirty," Bill would have said if he was there. But he wasn't, as Dixon walked away from a kid on his hands and knees crying. The other guy was dry-heaving into the rocks as Dixon got to his car. As he turned away from them both. He wondered what Bill was up to, right now. He wondered what his dad would have to say.

Cancer Zodiac Highlight

The Whirlwind's Reaping

Michael J. Shepley

Ivan settled back into his office chair. A real cushy roller. Seven Hundred bucks worth. What you can get when your office is the size of a studio apartment. In a mid-size city. Perks come with position.

So much better than in the days he inhabited a cubicle in a warehouse size space. With his mere BS tacked to a sideboard, and a few pictures of the few places he had been. A BS from Tinker Toy Tech, as he was often told.

Well, survival went to the swift and sure.

Those who learned early…

… taint what you know.

Ivan runs a hand over his eyes. Just for effect.

"So… you are trying to tell me… they are alive."

"Not exactly. Most are natural. Well… as far as we now know. But they have learned to mimic. Really well."

"To blend into nature."

"Exactly. Like they know we are here. And what we are."

The specimen of human sitting across from him was a prime example of what, back in the day, his Frat buddies would have called Nerd. And much worse, of course. A grind and computer cowboy who actually understood all the math instead of learning just the cues for a good guess. The latter via rote stimulus, a la Pavlov's pups. A Nerd that had survived to wizened face, 20th century wire rim glasses framing magnified fish eyes, bald pate, skinny of form, narrow of shoulders, topped in some sort of sporty horizontally banded earth tone short sleeve button down.

With pens, even pencils, protruding for a plastic pocket protector.

"No one's going to believe me telling that."

"3 Sigma certainty, so the Cray does say."

Ivan sighs. Then tries reason-

"It's GIGO. Depends on what you type in as initial parameters."

"Not so. The patterns never lie."

"Right. And I'm supposed to commit end of career suicide supporting this… analysis?"

"Our job is to study. Just pass my paper along as something come to your desk. Isn't that your job?"

Ivan shoots him killer eyes. A real laser blast. The Nerd immediately throws his eyes to the side, recognizing the waking of the alpha predator, before lamely whispering-

" Just saying..."

Yeah. One must keep the little people in line. Aware of who rules the roost. At all times. Or you get chaos. Still, the pencil neck would undoubtedly just run the thing over his head if he sat on it. Can't have that. Would wake the predators above Ivan.

"So, just to be clear here… Their process to gather, well... sustenance… is to flush insects up out of the fields..."

"And forests, or maybe just sparser open woods, made up of deciduous."

"And then they suck all the bugs in, straight out of the air, to ingest..."

"Yep, kinda like the way Baleen whales get plankton. Huge gulps."

"Dr. Pepper..."

"Popper, sir."

"The whole tale is bad fiction."

"But perfect science. Everything has tested out. Multiple times. The only way we..."

"You."

"Could have it wrong is if the initial data was skewed somehow. The same way, every time, everywhere..."

"All at once."

"Exactly."

Ivan suspects Dr. Popper never caught the flick. Nerds. Oblivious.

"Ok, and your answer is?"

"Answer… to what question?"

"Fine, to the problem."

"Is it a problem?"

Ivan gives him another laser blast. Then slowly says-

"You don't think, upstairs of upstairs, this isn't going to be defined as a problem?"

The Dr. diverts his eyes again.

"You bet it is. So just believe me here."

Silence. Then a resigned-

"Sure."

More silence as Ivan eyes his prey, sizing up the way to make the kill. He switches to a steely stern voice-

"Here's how we handle this. For right now, it's all classified. Not a word that these whirlwinds are … critters."

"Mimic tornadoes, that is the term we used. Most tornadoes are just what they seem. We think maybe there are a couple dozen mimics..."

Ivan continues as if there were no interruption-

"… going into feeding frenzies all over the place."

More silence. Then, continuing-

"You can see how that would lead to a herd of scorched cats. Running amok all over the place. Out of control… in the streets..."

"Yes. Yes, I see that..."

"So. Go back. Lock up the data. Get it all in a thumb. Delete the rest. And get the thumb back to me."

"Aw... right."

The Dr sounded hesitant.

"In one hour."

Silence.

Ivan gives the Dr. a last harsh look. Then growls-

"Go already."

And the Dr. flees. No look back.

Ivan sighs again. Picks up the desk phone and hits a speed dial. Waits through rings, then.

"Yellow."

"Popper."

"What?"

"We need to get him… um, into an institution."

"That far gone, eh?"

"I tried to talk reason. Hopeless..."

"Ok. Call the butterfly guys. On my authorization. Code word- conspiracy theory."

"The usual protocol then."

"Yeh… but… are you absolutely sure? Sooner or later we are gonna run into questioning families. With lawyers..."

"Don't worry with this one. I'll have all his shit in my hands in an hour, or so."

"Great, but… are you absolutely sure?"

"Yes, Eric. I know he knows. Proof positive."

Silence on the line. So Ivan goes on-

"He KNOWS."

"Ok. Just do it. Shut it all down."

Let Me Be Remembered As This

Holly Amber Webb

Put me on the list.
I will not censor my poetry, my voice, for anyone's
comfort.
Put me on a list.
You're telling me a sequence of words about how
the American flag on the moon is a symbol of
imperialism
triggered your fragile conservatism? That's fine.
Put me on a list.
My poem about the planning of the revolution was
flagged on rednote?
Like I care.
Put me on a list.
I'm earning my name on lists like anarchist girl
scout badges.
Let me be remembered as a political poet,
an outspoken poet,
a poet who voices her truth,
even if that earns my name on lists.
I don't care.
I will keep writing political poetry.
Isn't all poetry, all art, political?
Exactly.
Put me on that fucking list.

I'm No Longer Interested in Preserving a Man's Honor

Holly Amber Webb

How do you write about a crime committed?
How do you write about a crime committed with
your own body?
Some days I feel like a piece of evidence collecting
dust,
in an unmarked box in the back of a precinct,
lights flickering,
water stains on the ceiling to reflect the coffee
stains on the floor.
I sometimes wonder if I should have pressed
charges,
if I should have filed a police report,
but I've never had much faith in the justice system.
What justice would be brought to a situation
where the man claims it was consensual?
In our world, a man whispering a lie is more likely
to be believed
than a woman screaming the truth.
Too bad I'll scream anyway.
Writing about it,
being vulnerable enough to share my work on the
internet,
is me screaming about it.
He doesn't want the world to know what he did,
does not want me telling you all the truth.

It would destroy the image he has of himself, his
so-called honor.
Well that's too bad.
I've never considered the feelings of any man who's
done me wrong,
and I'm not about to start now.
How do you write about a crime committed?
Like this.

July Full Moon Special

Journey

Marlowe Blaire

In the quiet hours of dawn, she stands alone upon
the edge of the world,
her eyes tracing the faint horizon where sky and sea
dissolve into a whisper of color.
Each morning, she waits—silent, patient, hopeful—
though hope feels like a fragile thread unraveling
beneath her fingertips.

Her name is Elara, a woman of gentle grace and
quiet strength,
whose heart beats with a longing that echoes
through the vast emptiness of her days.
She carries within her a story—a story of love
sought across distant lands,
of promises made beneath stars that shimmered like
distant memories,
of dreams woven into the fabric of her soul, fragile
yet unbreakable.

She remembers the first time she saw him—an
apparition in a crowded marketplace,
a fleeting glance that caught her breath and held it
hostage in her chest.

His eyes, dark pools of mystery, beckoned her with
unspoken truths,
and in that moment, she believed their paths were
destined to intertwine.

They exchanged words like delicate whispers—soft,
tentative, full of unspoken promises—
but life, in its relentless march, kept them apart,
separating them by miles of doubt, by oceans of
circumstance.
She sent letters wrapped in hopes, but they returned
unopened,
their ink fading into the silence of unanswered
questions.

Elara roams through memories, her mind a tapestry
of shared moments—
the laughter that danced like fireflies in the night,
the silent embraces in the quiet hours when the
world was still,
the promises whispered under moonlit skies, fragile
as glass.
Yet, each memory is tinged with the ache of
absence,
a reminder of what remains forever just beyond
reach.

She walks through forests dense with shadows,
each step a testament to her unwavering search,
her heart a compass that points toward an elusive
horizon.
In her solitude, she finds solace in the wind that
carries his name,
in the songs of distant birds that seem to echo her
longing,

and in the silent prayers she offers to the stars—
hopes cast into the vast darkness.

Years pass like seasons shifting in their silent
rhythm,
and still she holds onto the flicker of hope,
though doubt sometimes clouds her vision,
and despair whispers softly in her ear.
Yet, she refuses to abandon the dream,
for love, she believes, is a fire that cannot be
extinguished,
even when it burns low, even when it flickers on the
verge of dying out.

One day, perhaps, she will find him—
or perhaps she will come to understand that love is
not always about finding,
but about becoming—becoming the story she
cherishes,
the hope she nurtures,
the strength she finds in the ache of longing.

Until then, she stands on the edge of the world,
a solitary figure against the vast, endless sky,
her heart beating softly in the quiet dawn,
holding onto a love that may never be fully realized,
but forever lives within her—an eternal whisper in
the wind.

Devotion

T. B. Vittini

—and so
every Tuesday morning

she rode the same quiet carriage
beyond the hollowed out
mountain range where dust

and dead leaves once fell
upon the West Wind's daughter
to be by her mother's side.

A handful
of fresh cut flowers arranged

on the windowsill each time—
the sweet fragrance they filled
the whole room with.

Slow attentive spoonfuls of
homemade purée. The gentle caress
of a sky blue linen napkin.

—and in
the waning candlelight

of Mary's room—in the hour of
her final breath—her daughter's hands
tenderly kneading the arches

of her frail feet; a calm
familiar voice safely carrying her
to where she had to go.

true pleasure

Daniel Frears

Wallace had seen all of the candidates for the day and his head was banging out a steady rhythm; an acute ache compounded by the sharp fluorescent lighting in the room. Whilst it thumped away his colleagues were making jokes about some of those they'd seen; mocking their answers, their mannerisms and even their clothes. Wallace looked over the suits the two of them were wearing and then down at his own, the pinstripe tie as good as invisible in its complete lack of character. The human capacity for hypocrisy never failed to amaze him, and fittingly he resolved to never again deride anyone in such a vulnerable position, especially for something as trivial as their fashion sense. Otis was one of the managers drafted in from another department to provide an impartial view of the candidates as was company policy, the idea being that he could judge their attributes and personality without the prospective bias of having to work with them.

"The guy was nearly shaking, and the answer he gave to question..." leaning back on the chair like a petulant child his bloated hands poked out from an ill-fitting grey suit framing an almost comically round belly, pushing open the gaps between the buttons of his shirt like blinking eyes. He flicked through the interview guide in a careless manner, his whole aspect suggesting contempt for the process he'd been requested to take part in. This grossly fat man felt superior to the candidates he held sway over, he ridiculed the questions, deeming

them 'outdated' and 'irrelevant' and surely considered himself better than Wallace as well.
"... four, question four. What kind of idiot gives an example like that? I don't know about you two, but that's when I stopped listening to what he was saying."
The delivery was intended to be comedic and Mark, the other interviewer and Wallace's fellow supervisor on their team, gave a noncommittal chuckle. Wallace let out an internal sigh as his head raged on unabated. Maybe this was hell? These 40 something year old men continued ragging on any little thing they could use as a tool for belittlement until finally they were done. Quite without realizing it Wallace had nodded and 'mmhmmed' his way through the whole deliberation process, and as a result of their arbitrary scoring they were in fact set to hire someone. He struggled to bring Elaine Sharples face to mind, though he was sure she did exist. The three men stood up with creaky grunts and groans, shook hands outside of the meeting room and went their separate ways. Thank god it was 5pm, thought Wallace.

The pain in his head followed him through the building, out into the carpark and onto the motorway for the drive home. It was a vexing presence more than a debilitating one with Wallace imagining a cruel fate in which it became his existing condition. At least my mind would be kept busy, he thought, there'd be no room for boredom or languishing on fretful existential matters, contentment being found in simply completing his daily functions whilst trying to mute the constant thudding. Surely anymore than that wouldn't be expected of him. By the time he was home the headache had subsided to a point of background noise, realizing the last half of the drive had been spent floating around his usual head spaces of 'what's for dinner', or 'when will I find time to cut the grass'. He'd been relieved of the burden which could have been his savior.

Six weeks had passed since the headache began and Elaine Sharples had been on their team for the last two. Wallace was assigned the role of 'managing her integration' which could be equated to babysitting, but he tried not to see it that way. Regardless, she was smart and didn't require any hand holding, getting to grips with the job in no time. With one of his main commitments all but taking care of itself Wallace had plenty of time on his hands, but with that came the extra space to dwell on his still aching head and a mounting issue with his partner, Simone. Simone, he really loved that name. It had such a sultry ring to it and she embodied the sound of Simone almost perfectly; dark haired, green eyed, languid in her movements, unpredictable in her behaviors, she was indeed the most Simone of all beings. Sitting idly at his desk Wallace couldn't help listing the stresses he faced, most of which were self-made of course and of little consequence when placed against the truly bothersome one; his inability to orgasm. This was the area into which so much of his mental capacity was going these days, and any amount of administrative work or staff development related initiatives were unable to wrest his attention for long. Why on earth couldn't he orgasm? His sex life had been pretty standard as far as he was concerned, having been with multiple partners, some of which were a one-off, some that lasted a few weeks and the few longer-term relationships he'd had. With different people came different experiences as in any other walk of life, confident with some and out of his depth with others. Wallace's personal circumstances often dictated the level of pleasure he was able to experience and thus impart, but overall, gradually, he had become a better lover, or so he thought. The problem now was that he couldn't orgasm despite months of very good sex. In the early stages of his intimacy with Simone he had ignored it, deciding that their precise chemistry was new and susceptible to the unexpected. It would change, he resolved. Their connection grew, and with this their freedom in and out of the bedroom, sharing experiences that had both of them reaching a climax but with something remaining unequivocally wrong. Wallace realized he had been mislabeling the phenomenon, for his body was in fact reacting in the way he expected it to; it would tingle, shake, tighten, release, relax but all the while he wouldn't *feel* a thing. He could as well be taking a sip of tea or watching an advertisement on TV for all of the mental detachment as his body reached climax. Simone would get her kicks sometimes, not all the time, but when she did her body would shudder with abandon, her rapturous noises matching suitably erratic movements before flopping into a post-euphoric state, her limbs a beautiful jelly, her features bathed in pure and absolute pleasure. Meanwhile Wallace would feel not a thing, knowing only that a physiological reaction had taken place but nothing more. The first time he had gotten off and was introduced to this

void of feeling he didn't sweat it. Despite it never
having happened before there were always firsts in
life and he paid it no more mind than he would
seeing a new car parked in the driveway next door.
When it happened a second and third time Wallace
paid more attention and there began his puzzlement.
The fourth time he and Simone were eye to eye, she
wrapped around him, he enveloped by her. His
body went into the uncontrolled jerks and quakes
with which he was familiar but this time he
reckoned Simone had sensed the disconnect.
Whether through an emptiness in his eyes or some
other intuition he feared that she knew there was a
piece missing, an integral piece which she couldn't
yet fathom. Neither made mention of *it* though the
seed was planted and from that day on the elephant
began growing in size.

Wallace stewed at his desk and all the while the
hum of his aching head continued, seeming
somehow married to the predicament. When he
thought about Simone there was nothing but
fondness, when he was with her he could become
excited by the faintest of touch, even a well placed
whisper enough to get him going. He scanned the
faces and bodies around the office trying to inspire
a similar intensity, digging for a lust he didn't
believe in but desperately wanted to identify,
hoping in vain that it would provide a clue to the
riddle. Wallace was ashamed to be analyzing people
like this, as though they were animals on show, but
he couldn't help it.
Jan? No. Tristan? No. Tanya? They'd had a thing
years ago when he'd first started which lasted a
couple of months, the initial intrigue giving way to

mundanity very quickly. She now represented little
more than an office fixture to Wallace, but, he
reflected, he'd always felt electric with her when
that time came. Again it was impossible to
reconcile so many factors that made so little sense
and his spirits slumped further.
Across the floor Elaine was sitting in a quiet corner
completing some training materials and Wallace
dragged himself from his torpor to check on her
progress, as his role demanded, and quite aside
from his intrusive thoughts.
"How're you getting on?" Wallace offered as he
rolled a chair up next to her, his tone perfunctory,
his face sporting the placid smile of supervisor-
cum-colleague.
"Ugh, health and safety inductions. Sure it's
important to know that Agnes from accounting is a
fire warden, and god forbid me knowing where the
defibrillator is actually ever matters, but this is
borrrrriiiiing." Elaine dragged the last word out
with a long, slow roll of her eyes. Wallace
registered that she didn't have the same work
persona that many others seemed to display, that of
switching into a robotic autopilot setting once they
crossed the threshold from personal to professional
life, character deemed surplus to requirements.
Elaine must have seen the contemplation in his
expression and tightened for a second, perhaps in
anticipation of a scolding. Instead Wallace smiled, a
broad and genuine smile reflecting the momentary
escape from his personal woes.
"Turns out that Agnes has actually hidden the defib,
so don't worry about having to shoulder that
burden." at which Elaine laughed and loosened
again. The clock showed just past midday. "You

can take your lunch now if you like? Give you a break from the fun."

"Sure, why not. Any recommendations around here? I've run out of leftovers so it's time for me to dip my toes into the world of paying for lunch." Wallace's mind went blank, immediately associating this with the social pressure that came alongside caring about someone's opinion. What do I eat? Wallace asked himself. Now, which of those options paints me as a man with good taste that also looks after himself but isn't too snobby about food? The few seconds of musing brought him to the place he'd known he would end up.

"Let's go to Lloyd's." he said standing. "Best sandwiches in town."

Wallace lowered himself into the bath, regretting not testing the temperature once his buttocks touched the water but continuing to submerge until the lower half of his body screamed violently. 'I'm subjecting myself to this' he said as way of explanation. 'My body will thank me' Once the shock had subsided he slid down for his chest to be swallowed by the scalding liquid, exhaling and finding peace in the red-hot embrace. His headache had retreated for the entire afternoon but was now back in its familiar spot, the heavy grasp squeezing his brain like a stubborn lemon. The time with Elaine had offered a reprieve, and reflecting on it now an appreciation of being untroubled; his head either not aching or suppressed to a near equivalent relief. He would never allow himself these thoughts if Simone were home with him, but she was away for a week with her work, thus Wallace indulged the memories of earlier that

day, the looks Elaine had given him, the ease with
which they had been with one another. His body
was a soft, pink, shimmering mass below the water
and above it steam rose in thick columns to be
pushed apart on reaching the ceiling, separating into
different bodies and running sleekly along the
surface. He followed the forms until they
evaporated and others took their place bringing on a
borderline state of hypnosis, sweat beading on his
forehead, his vision becoming affected by a mixture
of the vapor and a growing lightheadedness. In his
blurry illusions he imagined Elaine opposite, her
obscured features a merging of expressions, her
body round and white and inviting above the
waterline. An idea seeped into Wallace's rolling
thoughts, drifting away with the steam and coming
back to him over and over again to assert itself. His
dilemma was entirely a mystery, and mystery is
difficult to deal with, he reasoned. If he were to
pursue a simple experiment that gave immediate
and definitive results then all of the mystery could
be stripped away in an instant, and whilst it might
not solve the issue it could provide the clarity that
he, and he was sure Simone too, desired. The
question was *how?*

Another fortnight passed and the headache was still
there, simmering. Simone had been back a week,
and whilst their daily life was the usual blend of
love and companionship the weight of the situation
was clearly oppressing them; both only able to
forget about it for so long before a sexual reference
on the TV or some off the cuff comment would
lump them back in the mire of uncertainty. For the
week of Simone's absence Wallace had spent nights

in contemplation, turning over the different ways in which he could tell her his plan, as ridiculous as it seemed when he said it out loud.

"So babe, I'm pretty sure we both know that something strange is happening, and I don't know why it's this way. I'm certain it isn't anything you're doing, or not doing, so I'm at a loss, and I think that the only way I can figure this out is if I have sex with Elaine from work - yes, she's the new one.. yes, I am technically her boss etc - and see what happens."

Wallace tried wording it several ways and each version sounded ridiculous. Maybe it was ridiculous. It could be that some ideas, sentences, or statements that formulate within oneself should never be vocalized, regardless of how logical or appropriate they may seem in their own niche context; the distance between cognizance and speech sometimes presenting an unbridgeable gap. If he wasn't going to tell Simone then his options were to leave it all together or take action and deal with the consequences as they arose. Fundamentally he thought that finding a solution regardless of the means would constitute success, and even though Simone might struggle with his methods she'd be accepting of the intention and subsequent result. However, if it turned out that he was none the wiser after sleeping with his rather attractive and increasingly tempting colleague then his actions would likely come across as nothing short of careless cheating. The more Wallace thought about it the further he was from a decision, so he made up his mind to stop thinking and just do. During that week alone he'd had lunch with Elaine everyday, and for better or worse (for worse, of course) heads were starting to turn in the office. The gazes of usually distant colleagues turned from glassy eyed to full of intrigue and he was sure that the rumor mill was in full effect; speculation becoming interpretation, the interpretations being embellished and creating fully fledged tales to be spread around the place. Such was his growing attraction to Elaine that he couldn't find the impetus to care about what was being said, understanding that he was adopting an Elaine recklessness which was easier to accept when placed against his Simone futility.

That Friday after work Wallace abandoned his scruples and went headlong into the post work drinks that were taking place, that he knew Elaine would be attending and that he knew he could use to make good his plan. At the bar they were joined at the hip, neither of them shy to put a hand on the other or press close to share a whisper. Everyone in attendance acted as if there was nothing out of the ordinary, none of them asked about Simone or even registered the fact that Wallace had a partner and he thought how rotten the lot of them were to exhibit such cowardice, or worse indifference. Aside from the fact that the infidelity was his, shouldn't they too be showing a stronger set of morals? Shouldn't one of them pull him aside and ask what he's playing at running around like a newly single teenager? Of course these questions didn't bother him for long as he made sure to drink enough that all inhibitions were well skewed and duly left the bar with Elaine as soon as she invited him back to her place a short walk away. The air had that static kind of cold that comes with a clear night and no wind to affect their rising breath. They shuffled

along, shielded by their drunken warmth when
Wallace was hit with something unexpected. Their
fingers were intertwined when they weren't
touching each other's backs, hips or legs, clearly
painting the image of pure guilt, but instead of
anticipatory shame for the act he was about to
commit he felt deeply that *he* was a victim. The
perplexity that had multiplied with every bout of his
misfiring with Simone had congealed into a huge
mass hanging before him like an awfully grotesque
mirror, projecting his own ineptitude back at him.
Wallace wanted terribly for Simone to be happy and
instantly the tingle he had felt at Elaine's touch
vanished, her straying hands now as unwelcome as
a snake slithering up and down his spine that forced
him to shape his expression into a mask of pleasure
sitting atop a newly barren, deadened landscape.
"Elaine. I'm sorry, I can't do this. I have a partner
that I love and I've let this get out of hand."
Wallace stopped and turned to face Elaine, her hand
falling limp by her side at his sudden proclamation.
"I think you're great, really, but I've made a
mistake trying to convince myself that I'm solving
an issue by doing something that would only make
it worse." he was panting as he spoke, the words
coming in sharp torrents, and even as he did so he
was doubting himself, plumbing the depths of a
complete lack of conviction. Elaine's expression
was blank, regarding him in his fraught state with a
polar coolness. Wallace wasn't sure that he had
anymore to say, so there they stood for a moment,
his stabs of breath pumping out like a steam train,
Elaine's little more than a smooth chimney trickle.
"That is a shame." she said vacantly. Wallace
waited for more and imagined how he looked right

now, on tenterhooks, his whole body feeling like it had clenched up to the size of a fist.

"Don't worry. I'm not far from here." and she took the first steps away from Wallace who was frozen to the spot. As she turned her back he felt a wave of relief wash over him, his muscles loosening and a calm flow beginning to course from his head downwards. A few meters away Elaine stopped and turned around, her face showing a glowering determination.

"Actually, it's pretty fucking rude of you to just spring this on me. If you'd known from the start that this might happen then it would have been way more responsible of you to tell me, at least then *I* could have decided whether I wanted to keep going." she was now livid, her words well considered but pumped full of venom. "You've used me as some kind of toy, and now that you're feeling sorry for yourself, or scared you're tossing me aside. You should be ashamed of yourself. No-one with a scrap of decency would treat another person like this." at that she turned and fled, Wallace left wallowing in her cloud of fury. He had never felt so low as at that moment with all estimations of his character shattered in a way that he hadn't thought possible; to know that someone could bear such disdain for him made it all too real, his stomach a hopeless, sinking mass, his headache roaring back at full tilt to savage him. The air took on a painful quality that hadn't been present moments before so that his nostrils burned to draw it in, sending daggers upwards. Displaying all the hallmarks of an empty shell Wallace started on his way home.

The next morning was a drag. Wallace woke up to the insides of his skull churning like a slushy machine as best he could tell. Simone was gone by the time he opened his eyes and he was too forlorn to call out for her, lacking the heart to seek comfort from the one he'd failed so badly. Grabbing for his phone it duly spilled onto the floor. Things did not look good. On the other side of the wall the coffee machine rumbled away and Simone went about her routine as usual, the grinding and hissing providing her morning music whilst moving between the various stations; the sink to rinse her mug, the shelf to grab the sugar and back to the machine. From the bedroom came a clatter and she pictured Wallace languishing in his sad state, no doubt hungover given the thick, stale musk of alcohol she'd immediately fled. For a while now Simone had been considering what to do with their relationship, conflicted because of the steady satisfaction she still felt but which was becoming increasingly tempered by her emotional detachment, the bouts of discontentment slowly stripping the shine from the surfaces of their once pristine life together. She took the coffee through to the adjoining lounge and sat in front of the TV, turning it on to be greeted by the news channel. The news channel of all things. Whilst her own life moved through spells of disorder there were millions, probably billions that were going through trials far more desperate than her own, the luxurious couch and $2000 coffee machine an immediate testament to her relative affluence. She muted the TV and followed the silently shifting images of disaster and violence, humming a light melody as a vying attempt at serenity. A report on some far away conflict depicted scenes of a scorched landscape, closing in to two figures clad in layers of off-white material and face coverings wrapped tightly across their forehead, mouth and nose. An interviewer stood with the two men, both sporting rifles, and Simone tried to decipher the looks in their eyes, recognizing an eager shimmer that said excitement, doubt and fear all at once. She was similarly unconfident, she reflected, sipping at her lukewarm coffee. A loud yelping burst its way through the silence which Simone merely registered at first, her existential despondence permeating the strange moment. As it continued to change in pitch and volume she placed her coffee down and strolled to the bedroom, following her curiosity and lack of alarm to the source of commotion which was growing in intensity. Pushing open the bedroom door she was hit by the same claggy air as before and Wallace sat up against the headboard in the darkness. The curtains were still tightly drawn so that his phone screen offered the scant illumination pooling around him, a video playing and reflecting the rapidly changing light in his features. He was still wailing incomprehensibly before looking up to see Simone in the doorway.

"I've figured it out!" he yelled exultantly. "I've found out what's been happening with us."

"Happening with us?"

Wallace angled his phone downward to show the contents of his guts all over the sheets sprayed like confetti, splatter faintly visible on the walls and thick tendrils hung from the ceiling like party decorations.

"This is ridiculous." Simone was exasperated. How naive could he be to think this would get a reaction out of her?

"It's so... unnecessary."

Wallace had the painted smile of someone high on their own discovery, the cold screen glow still flashing against his pallid face.

"Are you going to clean all of this up?"

His expression unchanging she turned from the room leaving the door ajar, and sitting down with her now cold coffee the wailing started back up.

July New Moon Special

Celestial Bodies

Sawyer Hunter

In the velvet hush of night's embrace,
They dance, unchained, with effortless grace
Shining, twinkling—silent, bold
Secrets whispered, stories untold.

They drift across the midnight sky,
A fiery glow, a distant sigh
Movers of desire, celestial flame,
Their burning passion calls my name.

Stars that flicker, flicker bright,
Guiding lovers through the night
Their luminous touch, a gentle tease,
A cosmic dance, a sway, a tease.

In this vast universe of dreams,
Where nothing's ever as it seems
They spin, they glow, they softly call,
Bodies of light, and bodies—all.

Celestial bodies, vast and free,
In their allure, infinity
A universe both fierce and tender,
Where every spark ignites surrender.

The Hunt

John Martinez

EXT. BELMONT - 5:00 P.M. SATURDAY

Open in Belmont, an old fashioned, back country town in Appalachia, dirt roads snake through the landscape, with white painted houses lining the streets, the only vehicles are slightly rusted and practical, a mix of pickup trucks, old SUVs, and the occasional sedan. An expansive wood surrounds the town, merging into the towering hills. A main paved road bisects the town, along the road are various local businesses, a movie theater, a general store, a small restaurant, all owned by the townsfolk.

TOWNSFOLK rush along the dirt roads, ushering their children into their houses and closing the shutters as if preparing for a storm, but the sky is clear, dotted with white clouds. SHOPKEEPERS close their business, flipping the signs from "open" to "closed" and locking the doors. There is a distinct sense of urgency and methodology, they are

not unfamiliar to this routine.
The town is eerily quiet, cicadas
and gnats swarm the humid,
sweltering, dying summer air.

                              CUT TO:

INT. RURAL HOUSE - 5:30 P.M.
SATURDAY

Samuel (18, dressed in a plain
white t-shirt, jeans, and hiking
boots, with a backpack slung over
his back) and his FATHER (Late
40s to early 50s, dressed
similarly to his son) stand in
the living room of a rustic
house, similarly shuttered to
those seen before. Once garish,
now faded, furniture lines the
room, a large, out of place,
early-90s style home computer
sits unused in the corner of the
room.

Samuel's MOTHER (Late 40s to
early 50s, plump, wearing a faded
floral dress) fusses over Samuel
and his outfit, though there is
not much to fuss over. Samuel's
father buries himself in his
backpack, checking each item
methodically.

                MOTHER

                    Honey, let me grab a quick
                         picture.
Samuel's mother fumbles with a
small, teal digital camera, she
struggles to turn it on. Samuel
looks out the window as his mom
fusses over a loose strand of
hair.

                    MOTHER (CONT'D)
          Picked this up at the store the
          other day. I wanted to make sure
          I captured this forever! Oh, your
           aunts will be so happy to see
          you. Such a handsome young man.

                         SAMUEL
                    (uncomfortable)
           Mom, I wish you weren't always
                 taking pictures.

                         MOTHER
           It's not everyday a mother gets
            to see her little boy become a
                         man.

Samuel's mother kisses him on
the cheek. He tries to shrug
her off, but she hugs him
tighter.

                    MOTHER (CONT'D)
                    (whispering)
          I am so proud of you, Samuel.

Samuel's father looks up from
his backpack towards his wife
and son. He reaches for a rifle
sitting on the couch, and holds
it out to Samuel, now released
from his mother's grip.

                FATHER
      It's time to go, Sam.

                MOTHER
    Oh, you're not using that old
            thing, are you?

                FATHER
    I used it for my hunt, and my
      father before me. It'll be
      fine for Sam too, every boy
          needs a gun, dear.

Samuel's father hands Samuel the
rifle. He reluctantly takes it.

                        CUT TO:
EXT. BELMONT - 6:00 P.M. SATURDAY

Samuel and his father walk along
the dirt road towards the town
square. Samuel's mother stands on
the porch of their faded white
house, she holds the camera by
her side.

As they walk, other BOYS (all 17-18 and dressed similarly to Samuel) and their FATHERS (all ages, all manners of practical hunting clothing) exit their similarly shuttered houses, MOTHERS kiss their sons. Nondescript niceties and best wishes pepper the scene as the boys and their fathers begin to walk down the dirt road two by two. In total, there are approximately seven pairs of father and son.

A single crow flies low over Samuel's house. Its piercing "CAW" breaks the silence, then again, and then once more.

                    FATHER
          More kids than usual this year.

He looks to his son for a response, but Samuel is silent, looking straight ahead.

                    FATHER (CONT'D)
               Nervous?

                    SAMUEL
               A little.

Samuel's father looks at his son
with a new intensity.

                FATHER
      Don't be. You're my son.

                SAMUEL
      I know that Dad, it's just
              nerves.

Samuel and his father return to
their silence and continue down
the dirt road.

                              CUT TO:
EXT. TOWN SQUARE - 6:15 P.M.

Samuel, his father, the other
boys, and their fathers gather in
the town square. In total, there
are around twenty pairs. Each boy
grips a rifle in front of his
waist, perfectly bisecting the
center of his torso, his father
stands behind him, hands by his
side. The men make an orderly
formation facing the center of
the town square where an oxidized
copper statue of a long forgotten
founder sits, the face of the
statue is faded,
indistinguishable from a round,
shapeless mass.

The MAYOR stands in front of the statue and behind a wood podium. He checks names off a clipboard. Next to him stands his son, DAVIS (18, wearing a hard cast around his leg and leaning on crutches, well built and clearly athletic). On the podium sits a black box. Behind him there is a row of caged deer, each numbered on their flank with a violent red paint. One deer, an albino doe numbered "4," sits calmly in her cage.

                    MAYOR
     Well, it seems everyone's here.
He pauses.

                 MAYOR (CONT'D)
Record turnout if my memory serves
            me correct.

He waits for a response from the crowd, but none comes. He awkwardly laughs to himself. From the podium, he lifts up an old parchment sheet, a long antiquated looping script fills the page. The Mayor does not need it, he has the speech memorized, but for tradition's sake reads from the paper anyway.

MAYOR (CONT'D)
(reading from the paper)
Each one of you, the senior
boys of Belmont, must come
forward to the podium. From
there, you will randomly select
a slip of paper with a number
written on it.

The mayor gestures to the deer
behind him.

MAYOR (CONT'D)
(reading from the paper)
Your number corresponds to one of
these deer. At no later than six-
thirty, I will release the deer,
and at no later than seven, the
hunt will begin. You and your
fathers must bring back your
assigned deer no later than six
A.M. Monday.

The mayor pauses again, turns to
the crowd as if to ask them if
they have any questions, but
none come. The boys all stare
intently at the deer, as if
trying to size them up, no one
is particularly excited by the
ordeal.

MAYOR (CONT'D)
Well then, if there are no

                    questions, we'll begin the
                         drawing.

                                         CUT TO:

EXT. TOWN SQUARE - 6:20 P.M.

Samuel approaches the black box.
Around half of the boys have
already selected their deer. His
father stands behind him, the
mayor in front of him. He reaches
his hand into the box and draws a
slip of paper. He opens it, reads
it to himself, surveys the deer,
then hands it to the mayor.

                    MAYOR
                (to the crowd)
          Number four! The white doe!

The mayor gestures to the
doe in the cage, the doe
does not bother to look up.

                    MAYOR
                (to Samuel)
          You're lucky, that damn doe does
                nothing but sleep.

Samuel turns to look at the doe,
she sits calmly. He continues to
stare at the doe, after a short
while, she finally looks up, her
eyes meet Samuel's for a brief

                       130

moment, before she returns to her rest.

                    SAMUEL
              (to his father)
          It seems so calm.

                    FATHER
          They're calm animals.

Samuel glances back to the doe, but she does not return his gesture. He looks back to his father, expecting something more, but no words come. He motions for the two of them to exit the podium and they return to the formation.

                              CUT TO:

EXT. TOWN SQUARE - 6:30 P.M.

The last pair of father and son steps back from the podium, all numbers have been drawn. Davis continues to stand by his father's side. Unlike the other boys, he seems unbothered and does not hold a slip of paper. The boys maintain their formation.

                    MAYOR

Well, that concludes this year's
drawing. Good luck to all.

The mayor steps back, and one
by one releases each deer from
their cage. The deer dart off,
eyes wildly glancing back and
forth across the surroundings
as they exit from view and run
towards the woods. The white doe
runs with them, displaying a
new sense of urgency.

The boys watch silently as the
deer dart away, afraid to speak
or take their eyes off their
prey. As the deer break the
horizon, the silence is broken,
a new sense of perverse
excitement and anticipation
permeates the cooling air.

                    BOY
                (to Samuel)
         Isn't it weird Davis doesn't have
                  to hunt?.

                    FATHER
                  Davis?

                    SAMUEL
              (to his father)
           The mayor's son. School
                quarterback.

                    BOY
        I guess he hurt his leg, poor
          guy. We've got the big game
        coming up, he needs to be good to
                    play.

                  SAMUEL
              (disinterested)
          He seemed fine yesterday.

                  FATHER
        He should be hunting like the rest
                  of us.

The boy turns away from Samuel
and into another conversation.
Samuel and his father are left
isolated as the other boys and
their fathers begin to mingle.

                  FATHER
        Go talk to your friends, Sam.

                  SAMUEL
          I'm not sure if I'm in the
         mood for talking, a lot to
               think about.

                  FATHER
              Hmm. I see.

Samuel's father turns away
and goes to talk to the

other fathers. Samuel moves
to the outside of the group,
and sits under the shade of
a tree lining the town
square.

From his backpack, he takes a
sketchbook, he begins to sketch
the white doe. He becomes
engrossed in the work, and does
not look up as Davis approaches
him, hobbling on his crutches
and avoiding the occasional
stare from the crowd. He wishes
to
remain unseen, Samuel is the
perfect cover.

                DAVIS
   What are you drawing, Samuel?

Samuel turns the drawing towards
Davis.

                DAVIS
            Your deer?

Samuel nods, and looks back
down to the drawing. Davis
takes a seat next to Samuel,
laying his crutches beside him
and awkwardly stretching out
his "injured" leg.

            DAVIS (CONT'D)

                    (whispering)
          You know, I'm not really hurt.

Samuel sets his sketchbook
down, he sighs, then turns to
face Davis. His peace has been
broken.

                    SAMUEL
            I couldn't have guessed.

Davis takes Samuel's response
as a sign to continue, not
noticing the exasperation in
his voice. He drops his voice
low and leans closer to
Samuel.

                    DAVIS
                  (whispering)
          This whole hunt thing, it's
            too much work. I'm not
          risking a real injury chasing
          some stupid deer, and I'm not
                leaving Belmont.

                    SAMUEL
                   (dryly)
          So you pretended your leg was
                   broken?

                    DAVIS
                    Yep.

                    SAMUEL
                    (dryly)
But your leg was fine on Friday,
everyone saw you in school.

                    DAVIS
My dad believes me, and that's
            enough.

Samuel turns back to his
sketchbook. The two sit in
silence for a short while,
before Davis breaks in again.

                    DAVIS
You shouldn't draw the deer you
know. Don't want to get attached
          to the thing.

Samuel ignores him.

                    DAVIS
My older brother did his hunt a
few years back. He told me the
best thing to do is shoot it
right between the eyes.

Davis mimes a gun with his
fingers.

                DAVIS (CONT'D)
Bang! Right there, and it's dead.

Samuel looks up, then back to his
sketchbook.

                    SAMUEL
                    (dryly)
          Thanks for the advice.

Samuel sits in silence for a
moment.

                    DAVIS
        Y'know, hunting seems fun, but
        it's just not for me, I can't be
        bothered to track the thing down.
        If I wanted to kill a deer, it'd
        have to be fenced in. Maybe I
        should go to a hunting range.

Samuel looks up from his
sketchbook, he shuts it.

                    SAMUEL
                    (irritated)
          Well the rest of us have
          to hunt our deer here.
                    DAVIS
        Well I know that, I'm just saying.
             You're so uptight.

Samuel looks at Davis, he
considers a response, but does
not see a point. He grabs his

sketchbook, bag, and rifle, and
walks away.

                              CUT TO:

EXT. BELMONT - 7:15 P.M.

Samuel and his father walk along
a dirt road, side by side. Some
father-son pairs dot the street,
but the group is mostly
dispersed. The deer, long gone
now, are nowhere in sight.

The rifle is slung across
Samuel's shoulder
alongside his backpack.

                 SAMUEL
          So where do we start?

                 FATHER
       If I had to reckon, I'd say our
        best bet would be to check the
                 town first.

Samuel looks around, there are no
deer in sight. The majority of
the remaining pairs of father and
son are heading to the woods.

                 SAMUEL

It looks like everyone else is
headed to the woods. I think the
deer went there anyway.

FATHER
(more firmly)
They usually do, but we should
check the town first.

SAMUEL
Why? Let's get this over with, I
want to go home.

Samuel pauses for a second. He
has not told the truth, but his
father does not pick up on it.
FATHER
(clears throat, in a practiced
manner)
When I did the hunt, my father
and I checked every street before
we took a step into the woods,
and lo and behold, my deer was
curled up behind someone's shed.

Samuel looks at his father, then
back to the woods. He considers
arguing, but there is no point.

SAMUEL
(resigned)
Alright, let's start with the
town.

CUT TO:

EXT. BELMONT - 7:15-10:00 P.M. -
MONTAGE OF THE HUNT

Samuel and his father walk
along a dirt street of
Belmont, scanning each
house, there are no other
people, or deer.

GUNSHOT: The first pair of boy
and father walk out of the woods,
dragging their deer behind them.
The deer is unmistakably dead,
though its eyes show no
difference than when it was
alive. Its blood marks a crimson
trail behind them.

Samuel's mother watches from the
window as Samuel and his father
walk along their street. She
snaps another photo on the
digital camera.

GUNSHOT: A second pair of boy
and father walk out of the
woods, the boy carries his deer
triumphantly, unbothered by the
warm, crimson blood staining his
white shirt.

GUNSHOT: A boy and his father
bring a deer from a street

near Samuel and his father.
The boy nods as he walks past
Samuel. Samuel looks at the
deer with disgust.

Samuel and his father enter the
empty mainstreet, there are
clearly no deer, yet Samuel's
father continues down the
street. GUNSHOT. Samuel looks to
the woods.

GUNSHOT: From the small wooded
area near the school, a boy and
his father have found their deer.
The boy stands on top of the
dilapidated playset meant for the
younger students surveying his
kill. The deer's blood seeps deep
into the wood chips that line the
ground.

The sun sets in the sky,
brilliant purples, pinks,
oranges, and yellows paint a
sunset. GUNSHOT. the moon ushers
its way in, painting the sky a
deep black. Stars dot the sky.

GUNSHOT: A flock of birds fly
off the power lines, they head
to the woods.

More and more deer pile up in the
town square by the feet of the

statue of the founder, the mayor
tallies them up, checking names off
his list as more and more boys
complete the hunt.

GUNSHOT: From above, the dirt
roads of the town are lined with
bloody, crimson streaks. The same
pattern of crimson blood marks a
white shirt, a young girl watches
her mother scrub the blood out,
but the stain remains. The
mother's hands shake, the shirt
is ruined, but she still tries to
scrub out the blood. Her daughter
offers to help but the mother
waves her away.

GUNSHOT: The white doe sits in a
clearing. GUNSHOT, it turns its
head towards the sound. GUNSHOT,
but no one comes for it.

END MONTAGE OF THE HUNT

EXT. CAMP OUTSIDE THE WOODS -
10:15 P.M.

Samuel and his father sit around
a campfire, their sleeping rolls
laying behind them. An open flask
sits next to Samuel's father.
Night has truly fallen, it is
dark, with only the light of the
fire and stars illuminating the

pair. Ambient sounds from the birds and creatures of the woods and the crackling from the fire punctuate the eerie silence. Samuel is buried in his sketchbook, he is once again working to sketch the doe. His drawing is sleek, the deer is in motion, as if it is running off the page, trying to escape some unknown predator. He continues to sketch around the deer's figure, before finally putting the book down. Now he is the one to break the silence.

SAMUEL
Dad, is it bad we haven't found
the doe yet?

FATHER
Not necessarily, Sam. We have
until Monday.

SAMUEL
I know that, but won't the doe
only go further into the woods?
And the mountains, if it gets
there

FATHER
-It has to stop and sleep.

Samuel's father lays back along his sleeping roll.

The fire crackles, as Samuel prods at it with a stick. The rifle sits next to him, alongside his open sketchbook. He glances down at them, the fire light casts a dark shadow over the sketch.

                    SAMUEL
               Dad.

Samuel's father looks up.

                    SAMUEL (CONT'D)
          I'm not sure I can kill the doe.

                    FATHER
               Of course you can.

                    SAMUEL
               Well I was thinking…

                    FATHER
               (cutting in)
          That's the problem with your
                    generation.

Samuel laughs, but his father does not.

                    SAMUEL

144

I guess. But why do we do the
hunt in the first place? It
seems cruel to breed all these
deer just to…

Samuel trails off.

                    FATHER
It's a tradition… Don't tell me

you feel sympathy for the thing?

Samuel looks down at his sketch.

                    SAMUEL
I don't feel sympathy for it, but
     I don't want to kill it.

                    FATHER
Ridiculous, it's an animal, Sam.

                    SAMUEL
I know that… it doesn't mean I
   should want to kill it.

Samuel's father sits up, he
reaches for the flask, and
empties it into his mouth. Wiping
his lips with the back of his
hand, he turns to face Samuel.

                    FATHER

Long before you or I were
born, the men of this village
were weak.

Samuel's father spits.

                 FATHER (CONT'D)
          Belmont is no home to weak
          men, and you *should* never
          want to feel weak, Sam.

Samuel's father lies back down
and closes his eyes, no longer
interested in speaking to his
son.
                              CUT TO:

EXT. CAMP OUTSIDE THE WOODS -
11:00 P.M.

Samuel sits by the dying fire,
halfheartedly tending it with a
stick, his head nods up and
down, he begins to doze off.

As the embers burn out, he
catches a glimpse of white
fur against the backdrop
of the woods.

Samuel looks to the woods,
recognizing the shape of the
doe. He reaches to his side and
grabs the rifle. Fumbling with

the gun, he points it at the
doe. She looks back with her
quiet, flat eyes, she does not
seem alarmed by Samuel.

                    SAMUEL
                 (whispering)
                    Dad.

Not taking his eyes, or the
rifle, off the doe, Samuel
reaches over to wake his father,
but thinks better of it. He
recoils his hand and puts the
rifle on the ground. The doe nods
her head.

Quietly, Samuel gets up, he
smothers the fire, and creeps
over to the doe. He holds his
hand out to her. She places her
head against it, then turns and
slowly walks into the woods.

                         CUT TO:

EXT. CLEARING IN THE WOODS - 11:15
P.M.

Samuel and the doe emerge from a
path in the woods into an open
circular clearing. The moon
bathes the clearing in a cool
silver light, sparkling

moonflowers dot the edges of the clearing. The doe leads Samuel to the center, she curls up like a coin, resting in the slightly dewed grass, the light reflecting off her white pelt. Samuel surveys the clearing, then sits down next to the doe, he looks at her, and places his hand on her back.

                    SAMUEL
          My dad says, I
          need to kill you.
The doe turns her head towards Samuel. There is no warmth in the two black voids staring up at Samuel.

                    SAMUEL (CONT'D)
     I don't want to, but I have to.

Samuel begins to stroke the doe's pelt. She places her head back against the grass. She completes the round shape once again.

                    SAMUEL (CONT'D)
     You're so beautiful.

Samuel looks at the doe again, he begins to cry. He continues to stroke her pelt, burying his face into her softly rising and

falling body. After his tears
have dried, Samuel stands up,
looks back at the now sleeping
doe, and wordlessly exits the
clearing.

The doe stays in the clearing,
asleep, as night becomes day. She
doesn't stir as the sky begins to
darken with storm clouds, and
only looks up for a brief moment
when a pang of thunder breaks the
early morning's tranquility.

                              CUT TO:

EXT. CAMP OUTSIDE THE WOODS - 5:30
A.M.

Samuel's father awakes to see
Samuel sitting next to the now
extinguished fire. Samuel looks
disheveled; he clearly has not
slept. Samuel looks at his
father, the empty flask next to
his sleeping roll, and then
back to the ground. His
sketchbook is buried in his
bag, his father's rifle sits in
the dirt.

                    FATHER
          What time is it?

                    SAMUEL
                  Not sure.

Samuel's father reaches for the
flask next to him, he tries to
take a sip but finds it empty.

                    FATHER
                  Dammit.

Samuel looks up from the
ground and stares at his
father. He musters a courage
he has never felt before.

                    SAMUEL
          I'm not going to kill my doe.

Samuel's father ignores him, he
packs up his sleeping roll and
puts it in his bag. He looks to
the sky, dark storm clouds are
beginning to gather.

                    FATHER
               Looks like rain.

Samuel looks at his father, then
tries again.

                    SAMUEL
                (assertively)
            I'm not going to kill her.

Samuel's father, without
looking at Samuel, slams his
flask against the ground, and
takes the rifle. He then turns
to face Samuel, there is a calm
anger in his eyes.

                    FATHER
          Come on Sam. We're going to the
                    woods.

                    SAMUEL
               Dad...

Samuel's father jerks the
rifle upwards, first pointing
it at Samuel, then the woods.

                    FATHER
                              Grab your
                              things.
Samuel stares at his father,
then the rifle. He looks to
the woods, filled with a sense
of dread he has not felt since
his youth.

                              CUT TO:

EXT. TOWN SQUARE - 6:00 A.M.

The mayor and his daughter,
SCARLETT (18, traditionally north
eastern, a "proper" woman), stand

in the town square. A pile of the
dead deer lays at the feet of the
statue of the founder, its
shapeless face looks grotesque,
reflecting the mutilated, bloody
mass. Heavy, crimson blood lines
the recesses in the brickwork of
the town square, flies buzz
around the deer. Scarlett looks
at the pile with disgust, she is
clearly disturbed by what she
sees.

                MAYOR
        Almost everyone's done.

                SCARLETT
            (apprehensive)
          What about Bill?

The mayor checks his list.

                MAYOR
        He was the first one back.
        He's a good man, Scarlett, I
          wish you'd reconsider..

Scarlett looks at the pile of
deer then back to her father.
She ignores his comment about
Bill.

                SCARLETT

                    Dad, why do they have to do
                    this every year… kill the
                           deer I mean?

The mayor looks at Scarlett. His
face betrays nothing.

                    MAYOR
              I don't know.
A soft summer breeze cuts
through the square. The deer,
dead, seem to stir in the warm
air.

                              CUT TO:

EXT. WOODS - 6:15 A.M.

The dark clouds have continued to
gather in the sky, bathing the
woods in ominous dark tones.
Samuel and his father walk side
by side, the rifle still in his
father's hands. Various small
animals watch from the trees with
almost supernatural intrigue as
the pair trudge through the now
heavy undergrowth.

They continue to walk in silence
for some time, before finding
the path to the clearing Samuel
visited the prior night. Samuel
peers down the path, but the

dark shadows and creaking trees
refuse to reveal what the
clearing holds.

                    SAMUEL
                  (urgently)
         We should go left here.

                    FATHER
                  (forcefully)
         I say we go straight. Get out of
                the damn underbrush.

Samuel looks down the path
again, a tuft of white fur
sits in one of the thorny
bushes lining the side.

                    SAMUEL
         (matching his father's tone)
                We're going left.

Samuel's father looks to his son,
then down the path himself.

                    FATHER
             (lowering his voice)
         I said, we're going straight.
Samuel's father grabs Samuel by
the backpack strap resting on
his shoulders and tugs him
forward into the path. Samuel
almost trips, but regains his

balance and reluctantly follows
his father, two steps behind. A
clap of thunder breaks the sky.

As they walk, Samuel attempts to
look into the clearing, but is
unable to see what does, or does
not, reside in it. His father
trudges forward, with no regard
for remaining quiet. When they
reach the halfway point of the
path, Samuel's father stops,
holds up a single finger, and
continues forward, creeping with
the form of a practiced killer.

Rain begins to fall, the doe,
still curled into a coin like
shape, sleeps peacefully,
allowing the rain to wash away
the red "4" that marked her
flank. The red dye seeps into the
surrounding grass, giving the
illusion of pooling blood.

Samuel and his father enter the
clearing. The flowers are closed,
the sky is a dark, ominous gray.
The clearing is silent, the
animal sounds that punctuated the
trek through the forest are gone,
there is only the soft, rhythmic
sound of the rain.

Samuel's father hands Samuel the
rifle.

                    FATHER
                 (whispering)
            Shoot the deer, Sam.

Samuel looks to the doe.

                    SAMUEL
                     No.

                    FATHER
          Sam, you are my son. Shoot the
                    deer.

                    SAMUEL
             I won't do it.

                    FATHER
                 (forcefully)
                 Shoot it.

                    SAMUEL
          Dad, I can't do it. Last night I…

                    FATHER
          I don't give a damn about last
          night, I don't give a damn about
                  this deer…

Samuel's father looks at his son.
He pauses, surveying his face.

                    FATHER (CONT'D)
          Sam, I give a damn about you
              staying in Belmont.

Samuel looks at his father. He
looks back to the doe. He points
the rifle, considering the
possibility of pulling the
trigger, ending the ordeal,
leaving it dead.

Samuel lowers the rifle.

                    SAMUEL
          Dad, I can't do it, I can't kill
                      her...

Samuel tries to say more, but
his dad stops him, his
forceful nature is gone.

                    FATHER
          Then give me the rifle.

Samuel looks to his dad, then
to the doe. He points the
rifle towards the sky, holding
it across the center of his
body.

                    SAMUEL

No.

GUNSHOT. GUNSHOT. GUNSHOT.
Samuel shoots the rifle three
times, directly into the air. He
pulls the trigger a fourth time,
but the gun does not fire. Birds
fly out of the trees surrounding
the clearing, but the doe does
not stir. Samuel looks at her,
tears begin to stream down his
face, mixing with the now heavy
rain.
                    SAMUEL
                  (yelling)
     Run! Please! Run… run… run and
                   leave…

The doe does not stir. Samuel,
defeated, stops his protest and
breaks into quiet sobs.

Samuel's father puts his hand
on his son's shoulder. With
his other hand, he adjusts his
rifle, pointing it at the
doe.

                    FATHER
                  (quietly)
     Just pull the trigger. Please,
                    Sam.

The doe, finally awoken from her slumber, looks to Samuel. Her cold, black, dead eyes reflecting the rain. The red dye washed away from her body. She is pure white, almost shining against the darkened forest.

Samuel's father adjusts the rifle again, holding it up to his son's eyes. He forces Samuel to look through the sights, to see the barrel of the rifle aimed between the doe's eyes.

FATHER
There you go, right between the eyes.

Samuel looks at the doe. His tears have been washed away by the rain.

GUNSHOT.

The doe is dead, her blood pools on the ground, mixing with the red ink. She is disfigured, her head is smashed in, a disgusting image, not one of pride or honor. Samuel's father surveys the doe briefly, his face betrays a twinge of sickness.

Samuel's father looks back to his son, he too is bleeding. The rifle barrel is bent at an odd angle, sharp fragments of metal are missing. They have flown backwards into Samuel's head and neck. He places his fingers to his son's forehead, warm, viscous blood flows between them. The gun has catastrophically failed.

                    FATHER
                 Sam!

He drops to his knees, lowering Samuel's body down into his arms. Samuel's eyes open slightly, he looks up at his dad. His eyes are as cold as the doe's.

                    SAMUEL
              Did I kill her?

Samuel's father nods, his eyes start to tear up.

                    FATHER
You did Sam, I'm so proud of you.

Samuel coughs, he closes his eyes.

                    SAMUEL

I didn't want to.

Samuel dies.

                              CUT TO:

EXT. BELMONT - 9:00 A.M.

The rain has cleared. The sun
mercilessly beats down on the
town as the townsfolk begin to
return to normalcy. The hunt is
over.

From the woods, Samuel's father
walks back to the town. Slung
over his shoulder, he carries his
dead son. Behind him, he drags
the doe, now stained red with its
own blood, leaving a crimson
trail behind him.

                         FADE OUT

Leo Zodiac Highlight

Vibrance

Riley Phillips

Beneath a radiant sun, I stand tall,
My spirit blazing with a fierce warmth,
Drawing eyes with a natural glow,
A presence that commands attention and respect.

I thrive in the center of the room,
Seeking admiration not for vanity, but for the joy of
sharing my light,
A leader born from confidence, fueled by passion,
Guided by an inner fire that refuses to wane.

I carry a pride that fuels my ambitions,
A heart eager to inspire and be admired,
Yet beneath the strength, there's a tenderness,
A desire for genuine connection amid the applause.

I move with purpose, unafraid to stand out,
Embracing challenges as opportunities to shine
brighter,
Knowing that my warmth can ignite others,
And that my presence leaves a mark—resilient,
vibrant, unforgettable.

Violating the Honor Code at Annapolis

Kurt Schimdt

At eighteen, I'm too young to understand being accepted to Annapolis could become the curse that might break me. I'm leaving a traumatic childhood behind, moving to an unseen world in which hazing is a ritual meant to indoctrinate neophytes into an institution in which the uniform itself is a symbol of power and grandeur. I've heard enough from reliable sources to fear hazing by the upperclassmen but am oblivious to the possibility new trauma may regenerate old trauma. I am oblivious to the loss of identity.

During plebe indoctrination summer at Annapolis, we neophytes run everywhere and practice marching with an M1 rifle in the hot July sun. I wonder why a Navy guy needs to learn to carry a rifle. We shower off the sweat, change uniforms, and sprint to the next formation — a perpetual race against an immovable clock.

At our table in the mess hall, the midshipman in charge of plebe summer supervision says we'll have to brace up during meals when the brigade returns in September, saying that's when the shit will hit the fan. He advises us to memorize *Reef Points*, which is a small black bible of naval history, obscure facts, and stupid speeches you have to recite if prompted. I see that *Reef Points* defines a "sand blower" as "he who walks at a low altitude." That there is no special definition for a big guy implies that sand blowers are a scrutinized minority. I am only 5' 4".

The upperclassmen return to Annapolis from their summer cruises and begin the bullshit. I am at the mercy of foul-mouthed overseers who think I need to "straighten up and fly right." I know what a maniac is all about. I've heard the maniac voice a thousand times. I've seen the maniac blood vessels bulging in my father's neck. It's scary.

In the mess hall the overseers shout at me as though I am unwelcome in my new home. If they dislike my answers to their questions or my recitations from *Reef Points*, they make me "shove out," which means pushing my chair away while maintaining the sitting position. When my legs begin aching, I start sinking. It's difficult to eat when my legs ache and my chin is almost level with the edge of the table. They don't say "come aboard" until my legs are almost gone. Most overseers say "come around" to their room ten minutes past reveille, which means getting up at O-five-forty-five to shower and shave and brush up on answers to questions. This is what I fear most, because I'm unsure what will happen in a room with some deranged Second Classman who has been waiting an entire year for his first opportunity to haze plebes.

I see craziness in some of their eyes. When an upperclassman sticks his face up close to mine, I see a few with the normal eyes and the normal smile. I see others with the evil eyes and grim mouth — my father all over again.

The one who worries me most is a snowblower with a scary grin. Mister Beam. He rooms with Mister Bengston, whose face is a death mask, which is nerve-wracking too. Mister Beem's beady eyes drill right through me. He has an evil-looking grin, as if he is plotting something diabolical. He makes me come around with my M1 parade rifle and hold it vertically at arm's length above an overturned trash can until the heavy length of steel drops down with a clunk. Then he says I'm not going to make it at the Academy.

My two "wives" and I inhabit a small room with a bunk bed and a single, a double desk and a single, and three metal lockers. That our roommates are called "wives" gives the secret language a nuance that I could do without, especially since my father had an extra "wife" before my mother divorced him.

Joe does the most praying to God. After lights out each night, Joe fiddles with his rosary beads and mumbles Hail Marys and Our Fathers until Fred says he can say a couple for us and then knock it off so we can sleep. Joe should have saved his prayers for the tower.

The fifty-foot tower stands in the middle of the Natatorium's indoor swimming pool. As part of our Phys Ed swimming class, each plebe has to climb the tower and jump off into the pool. The instructor says, "When you get to the top, stand on the edge. Fold your arms across your chest like this. Put one hand over your mouth and hold your nose with your thumb and forefinger. Look straight ahead. Then step off and cross your legs like this. If you don't, you'll be a soprano when we fish you out."

Most of the class laughs, but not Joe. He can't swim.

Fred and I are among the first to climb the tower, wanting to get it over with quickly. You don't want to let the power of fear hang around until you're paralyzed. At the top, the scary thing is looking down. I look straight ahead, step off, and cross my legs. Can a tenor become a soprano? I knife into the water, immersed in a sea of bubbles. I swim up to the surface. At the edge of the pool I sit with Fred and watch other jumpers. When Joe's turn comes, he doesn't step off. His brown skin and black, brush-cut hair give him the appearance of a Comanche standing at the edge of a cliff looking for smoke signals that will provide guidance, although he is actually an ex-football jock who is not sure God will save him from the jump. He steps back from the edge and makes the sign of the cross. He folds his arms across his chest and pinches off his nose. He steps up to the edge. He looks straight ahead. He doesn't budge. Everybody shouts encouragement. Joe doesn't budge. Everybody starts betting whether he'll go or not. He finally steps off, and someone shouts, "Cross your legs!" Joe's collision with the water sends up a huge spray. Everyone says, "Oooooooo." Fred and I move to the spot where bubbles are rising. Joe surfaces with eyes that have seen Hell. He claws his way to the edge of the pool. Fred and I each grab one of his arms and ask if he is okay. Joe nods and gasps for air and says, "Hail-Mary-Mother-of-God."

I'm glad Joe survived the jump, because his girlfriend at a nursing school in Pennsylvania has lined me up with a date for the Army-Navy football game. And according to Joe, my date is "a sure thing." I take this to mean she has experience, and a nurse with sexual expertise is more than a virgin could ask for.

During the autumn chaos, I receive a letter from Mom saying she's married again. She describes a kind but uneducated man who runs an auto-body repair shop, has plans to fix up our house, and is eager to meet me when I come home for Christmas. I'm not particularly interested in meeting a stepfather but am more than ready for a reprieve from the verbal assaults that feel similar to those with which my father abused Mom for so many years.

···

After listening to classmates' discussions about their conquests, it is clear I am the only entering Fourth Classman who is still a virgin and doesn't know the location of a woman's clitoris. No one in my home ever discussed this part of a woman's anatomy.

I am ashamed to think I don't know what the clitoris is. From what Fred says about rubbing the crotch and starting the fire, I am guessing it is possibly inside the vagina. The female power button. If I don't know this, how can I love a woman properly? My date is experienced and will expect me to know what every good lover knows.

There is so much chaos the week before the big game I don't have time to worry about whether I can satisfy an experienced woman. I can barely satisfy the evil ones who have me running this way and that, screaming "Beat Army" at every turn in the corridor. The evil ones seem more agitated than usual, as if Armageddon is near, as if we are about to embark upon the war of all wars. The pep rallies are a frenzy of screaming animals that will devour the Army team once we arrive in the combat zone called Philadelphia. If we beat Army, there will be no plebe hazing for the three weeks leading up to Christmas leave. If we lose, the evil ones will take out the frustration of defeat on their slave plebes.

We ride to Philly in big buses. Navy hits the Army wall. We lose. I am frozen as much by the prospect of returning to Annapolis as I am by the biting wind in Memorial Stadium. At the final gun, we sing a dispirited "Navy Blue and Gold," and then everyone moves down to the field to meet their women.

Like most women on the field, our dates appear eventually in fancy overcoats and spike-heeled shoes that make little holes in the grass. I'm happy my date is attractive and small, because I'm prepared to accept almost any woman who is a sure thing. Lorraine's short hair is ash blonde, her eyes and smile are mischievous. Her only flaws are a thick nose and acne, which are actually a good sign if you believe those guys who say a poor complexion means a woman was oversexed. She asks questions about Annapolis and seems to like me.

We take a taxi to a restaurant. When I remove Lorraine's coat, I see a silk blouse that reveals a good figure. It is difficult to concentrate on the meal and small talk when I know the women have booze in their hotel room and we have a midnight curfew.

Later in the hotel room Lorraine says she is going to pour herself a bourbon and ginger ale and asks if she can make me one too. I say yes, and the taste is good. My jacket and tie and shoes are off, and I'm sitting on a woman's bed. Fred and his date are on another bed, Joe and his date are on the sofa. As Lorraine and I are sipping our drinks and getting to know one another, Joe goes around and turns off all the lights. So now Lorraine and I are drinking in the dark while Joe and his date go at one another on the sofa. It's difficult to concentrate on conversation with a date when you can hear the sounds of passion.

Lorraine giggles, puts her free hand on the back of my neck, and pulls us into a passionate first kiss. When our lips finally part, we place our drinks on the nightstand and go at one another with both hands. There can be no better heaven than being tangled up with Lorraine on this bed. When the legs are tangled together, there is incidental rubbing going on. Maybe I don't have to put my hand down there.

Soon we are naked in bed. I decide to touch the place that Fred says starts the furnace. It seems I've found the clitoris, because suddenly I am no longer a virgin.

As Lorraine and I are resting, I think about an encore. But an alarm goes off. Joe says, "We've got twenty minutes to get to the buses."

The three of us dress in the dark, and I'm having trouble finding all the uniform pieces. I've practiced getting into a uniform at jet speed, but never in the dark. I kiss Lorraine goodbye and promise to write and lurch out the door with Joe and Fred. On the elevator down, we keep adjusting pieces of our uniform. We sprint through the hotel lobby and the streets of Philadelphia until we see the buses lined up on the street that is the preordained pickup spot. We settle into seats on our bus. As the buses leave the city, I think how lovely a woman's body is and how wonderful it would have been to be in bed with Lorraine for more time than the Cinderella allowance.

*

Despite having no experience in wrestling, I decide to try out for the plebe team, which, during meals, has a training table where no hazing occurs. Where you don't have to sit braced up straight and looking straight ahead. I hate being at meals where a sadistic upperclassman waits until a morsel of food is almost to my lips before firing a question at me, requiring that I drop my fork immediately.

The bodies in the wrestling loft of MacDonough Hall are muscular and sweaty and smelling like ripe cheese. For my tryout I'm matched against an opponent who appears heavier and has experience written on his face. For awhile, I use my speed to skip away when he lunges for my legs, but suddenly I'm on my stomach with one leg bent up toward my back. The more I struggle to escape, the more he presses down on the doubled-up leg. The whistle blows finally. The match is over, and now there is some strange clicking in my knee. I limp to Misery Hall, where a corpsman applies an ice pack and tells me to hold it there for an hour. The next morning the knee is swollen, and after limping to a doctor consult in Sick Bay, I ride a Navy bus to the Academy hospital, where another doctor draws fluid from the knee with a gigantic hypodermic needle while I grip the examining table until my knuckles are white.

One week before the brigade's departure for Christmas leave, the rumor at breakfast is that today is when the doctors decide who can leave the hospital and go home for the holidays. I test my leg, and the knee is a fucking barrel of pain. But when the doctor arrives, I lie. "No pain, sir. And the swelling's almost gone."

"Okay," he says, "Let's see you get up and take
a little walk on it."

I hop off the bed and limp across the open ward
as fast as I can, hoping that speed makes up for the
limp.

"How's it feel?"

"Good, sir. Real good."

"Okay. Pack up your things and get out of
here."

•••

Mom and Ed and my sisters meet my train in
Brattleboro, Vermont, late on a frigid December
night. We pile into Ed's pale green Cadillac, which
is eight years old but shined bright as new.

Ed is a big Finn with a short crew cut, thick
middle, and little facial expression. His soft deep
voice speaks with authority when he reminds my
sisters about their chores. When Ed and I drink a
beer together, I see that he takes a shot of whiskey
with his beer, the dreaded boilermaker that Joe and
Fred warned me about. Ed seems like a kind and
gentle giant, but he is divorced too, so I wonder if
there are secrets hidden beneath the gentle facade.
When Mom asks him when he'll talk to Henry
about his broken sink drain that is allowing Henry's
gray water to exit the back of his rundown
farmhouse and flow down over our wall as it
freezes, Ed says, "Gosh, Liz, not during the
holidays. I'll speak to Henry after the holidays."

I can tell neither one of them wants to speak
with Henry about his sink drain, both wanting to
avoid a power struggle with Henry, who has a bad
temper and once used a pitchfork to chase a health
inspector off his property.

While I'm home, I don't tell anyone I'm afraid of upperclassmen who seem mentally unbalanced. When Ed asks about the plebe hazing, I say, "I can handle anything they can dish out." In truth, I feel as though the power structure has me in some sort of chokehold in which the fear of suffocating is worse than actual events.

...

Back in Annapolis after Christmas leave, the overseers make me shove out in the mess hall when my bad leg is still too painful for sitting on air. When I request permission to explain about the leg, they tell me to stop being a malingerer. When I try to put most of my weight on the good leg, I sink until my chin is level with my plate. Then usually one of the overseers says, "Come aboard."

Then one evening when my wives and I are studying, our door bangs open. An upperclassman in full dress says I need to get dressed and come with him. Something feels wrong. He doesn't say anything, just walks me through the corridors to an office where the duty officer, a lieutenant, sits behind a desk. He says, "There's been a death in your family. I don't know what relation he is to you, but Ed has died."

I feel immediate relief that it isn't Mom and then immediate guilt about my relief. "He's my stepfather."

He says, "I'm sorry. You can call your family from the inner office and arrange for emergency leave if you need to attend the funeral."

I call Mom, and she says Ed walked up to Henry's in the evening to talk about the sink drain. Henry swore at him and told him to get out of his yard, and when Ed started to walk back, he went

172

down. Mom says she'd been watching and listening from the side door. She says, "I knew he was gone as soon as he collapsed. The doctor told Ed he had heart problems and should give up drinking. But Ed was stubborn about having his drink each day."

"Do you want me to come home?"

"No, I just needed you to know. There's nothing you can do here. You need to stay there and concentrate on your studies."

"They told me I can come home for the funeral."

"I'd feel better if you stayed there."

"Ma, I'm real sorry about Ed."

"Me too, honey. Me too."

It is the persistent winter dampness blowing in from the Chesapeake Bay that makes the dark chill feel colder than my snowy old home. Mom doesn't say in her letters whether the cold and the aftermath of Ed's death depressed her in any way. She says only that Ed's dog, Davy Crockett, killed two of Henry's chickens, which seems like some measure of retribution. Mom doesn't say if she thinks Henry felt any remorse about taunting Ed as he lay dying, only that he fixed the sink drain quietly and has avoided her.

I suspect she feels that my becoming a success compensates for any bad luck she might be experiencing. But I have no idea what I'm becoming. I am aware that, even if I doubt my warrior destiny, I have to prove I don't quit when the going gets tough. It is best to avoid thinking beyond each day.

What's worse than the cold winds are the silent moods and unpredictability of the upperclassmen. I worry constantly about when one of those with my father's Jekyll-and-Hyde personality will strike next. And though the strikes become less frequent, rotating to a table in the dining hall where a sniper resides stimulates a fear that churns my stomach.

As spring approaches, the upperclassmen stop hazing, and I dream about the traditional Youngster Cruise to the Mediterranean and the French Riviera. But then the Academy announces that our cruise will be to the Great Lakes. Even so, I see our impending time on destroyers as emancipation from the chaos of Bancroft Hall.

...

In the middle of my third year a strange feeling seeps into me as silently as a virus. Life seems empty, as if someone turned the "off" switch in my head. It's another cold, damp winter in Annapolis. The blue skies that once lifted me seem dark.

I try to fulfill my duty to "indoctrinate" plebes, but chastising them for even small infractions makes me feel horrible. I hate using that power. So I stop.

I don't feel like studying anymore either. So I stop. It isn't really a conscious decision, just something that happens one night and continues to the next, as if something inside me has become disconnected. It seems as though my mind is becoming a dangerous place, a cesspool of illogical thoughts. That choking sensation I felt as a plebe has returned. I play Solitaire at my desk every night, one card on another card.

While apathy numbs me, I copy answers from a classmate's Leadership quiz in perhaps a subconscious rejection of the military leader's role and all the power that it entails. Someone notices and reports that I have violated the honor code.

174

Academy officials decide I'm not fulfilling my obligation as an honorable warrior in this privileged world and force me to resign. I suspect my mental shutdown and subsequent bad behavior was a provocation to have others make a decision that I couldn't make. I had stayed here too long, just as Mom had stayed too long with my father.

...

At the time of my dismissal, I found some small sense of vindication from Admiral Rickover's Congressional testimony that the Academy should be shut down or drastically improved. According to a news report then in the Washington Post, Rickover had said the Academy regimented its young men under English boarding school rules, fostering adolescence and encouraging a preoccupation with football, escort duty for beauty contestants, policing the quarters, and similar trivia. Rickover didn't mention the honor code or the stupidity of hazing, but I thought he implied it when he said they treat students like children and stifle interest in learning.

During the next ten years, I graduated from Michigan State University with a BSME, vagabonded around Europe for a year, took a writing course, and wrote a novel about plebe year at the Academy. Crown Publishers thought it would make a decent young adult novel, except for a few obscenities. The book earned good reviews from organizations like Publishers Weekly, Kirkus Reviews, Booklist, and the American Library Association. Two local newspapers interviewed me, took photographs of me on my front steps (one with my hound dog), and produced in-depth write-ups of my road to publication. I felt overjoyed at accomplishing this goal but disappointed with the lousy compensation that my writing instructor had predicted. I knew I had to find a better way to earn a living as a writer. By the time I was married and had a son, I'd established a well-paid career as a technical writer with two hi-tech companies.

But there was never anything as exciting in that career as seeing my name on the cover of a hard-bound novel. Or telling my version of the Annapolis adventure.

Last week they threw me out of Annapolis. Made me resign. The whole thing made me sick, because the Naval Academy had been an opportunity to make something out of myself, a chance to see the world—places like Barcelona. Now that it's all over, I don't know exactly what I'm going to do.

The Wars We Fought

Larena Nellies-Ortiz

Academic Honesty

Jeffery Johnson

Few have careers where you look forward to returning to work on Monday. For Scott Greene, the Monday high paled in comparison to the anticipation of returning to start the new school year in the fall. Scott wasn't pathological. He enjoyed his weekends just fine. And if truth be told, by the middle of the spring quarter, he always found himself eager for summer vacation.

Scott simply loved being a professor at a small liberal arts college. In what was usually intended as a putdown, he relished being the "sage on the stage." Sure, half of his audience on any given day looked bored, if not downright asleep. But he had learned very early on to focus on the other half. He could almost always find faces that found the ontological argument or the trolley problem fascinating. He took satisfaction in preparing his lectures and turning a new generation on to the wonders of analytical philosophy. Toulmin College was hardly a research institution, so the pressure to publish had never been a major professional concern. Still, he took great pride in his modest scholarly contributions to his discipline.

So, what was not to like? Most of his colleagues would have said the petty academic politics or grading papers. Scott, however, immensely enjoyed the give-and-take of shared governance, though he, often as not, found himself on the losing end of the issues he most cared about. No professor is going to say that they enjoy grading. But his glass-is-half-full personality rescued him here as well. The papers or essay exams that demonstrated fundamental understanding more than compensated for the drudgery of wading through the many that did not. Scott's problem was cheating.

He prided himself on being an honest man. Usually, the occasions were relatively trivial. Several times, he called service providers back to his table to correct mistakes on the check. Most of these were to the advantage of the restaurant. A forgotten beer here, a second glass of wine there. None of this resulted from some deeply religious upbringing or anything of that sort. All of this simply came naturally to him. Or perhaps it had something to do with karma. Once, he found a wallet on the subway. It contained over three hundred dollars. Using nothing but the information on the driver's license, he ascertained the owner's phone number and email address and arranged to meet and return it. Less than a year later, while on vacation in Virginia, he absent-mindedly put his own iPhone, which doubled as his wallet, on his rental car's roof as he pulled off an unnecessary sweater and promptly drove off. Miraculously, the phone, all of his credit cards, and cash arrived three weeks later in the mail, without so much as a how do you do, or the chance to thank his benefactor or offer a reward. So, why did lying, stealing, and cheating haunt his professorial life?

#

The year in North Dakota was a blur of exhaustion, exhilaration, and, ultimately, disenchantment. The disappointment was not receiving a tenure-track job offer. The weariness was the typical fate of most beginning professors, with new courses to create and prep for and a whole new work rhythm to adjust to. Being a professor was a lot harder than being a TA. But all of this was more than overshadowed by the pure joy of having secured his first job and the confident feeling that he was beginning his dreamed-about career.

The death penalty played a significant role in his Contemporary Moral Problems course. Emily Cranor's term paper started promisingly. She had obviously done the reading and understood some of the finer points in the controversy Scott had labored to bring out in his lectures. But something nagged in the back of his mind. Wasn't this paper not just good, but too good? In graduate school, Scott had learned a nifty trick to track down plagiarism. He went to his trusty Google page and picked a particularly professional-sounding section from Emily's paper. He then started a search. The very first hit was a Wikipedia article on capital punishment. The suspicious passage was right there in so many words. But the real bonus was in the citations the online author had included. Several were classics that Scott instantly recognized, but the one that caught his eye was "Three Problems with Capital Punishment," the exact title of Emily's paper. Sure enough, she had simply stolen the first half of the relatively obscure scholar's article.

This was a problem three times over. As a TA, plagiarism was not his direct responsibility but that of the professor whose course he was assisting in. He would simply report his suspicions, and that was pretty much the end of the matter, at least as far as he was concerned. Now, however, this was definitely his problem, and he had no idea what his strategy for cheating was going to be. A stern warning? An F on the assignment? Failure in the course? Or a formal disciplinary charge with a recommendation for expulsion? To make matters worse, Scott had no idea what Central North Dakota State's academic honesty policy was. But all this paled in comparison to the real dilemma.

Emily Cranor was no ordinary student. She was the fiancée of one of Scott's new colleagues. Indeed, Emily and George had invited him to dinner to welcome him to the Division of Arts and Letters. What in God's name was he supposed to do now? At a purely pragmatic level, the answer was obvious. Just ignore everything and give Emily her ill-gotten A. The last thing he needed when he desperately wanted a permanent job offer was to make enemies. To his profound shame, he seriously considered this option. But in the end, he found himself more offended that Emily had put him in such an untenable position than he was professionally circumspect. What the hell? He made the appointment to see his new division chair.

Donald Singer was a thoughtful man, and he immediately saw the predicament. "Well, damn, Scott, this is something of a cluster fuck, isn't it? You can do whatever your conscience dictates. You'll have the full support of my office. I have to tell you, though, George Scanlon is going to have a shitfit. For the sake of peace in the Division, I wish we could find some less confrontational way of dealing with this."

Scott sadly smiled. "I appreciate your backing, and I totally understand your concerns. If I'm honest, I don't even know what my conscience dictates. Do you have any suggestions?"

"I'm going to be more than a little indiscreet here," Singer began. "I hope you will keep this between the two of us. George needs to know about this. It's been less than two years since his divorce. I like Emily just fine, but she's reckless. What the fuck was she thinking? With your permission, I'd like to inform George about what's happened. I'll tell him Emily must withdraw from your course. The two of them can figure things out from there. How does that sound?"

Scott merely offered a sad nod. My God, the realization hit him. That's a much greater price to pay than an F on the paper or even an F in the course. We're fucking with someone's marriage. Well, at least future marriage. Is this what he really wanted? Maybe Dr. Singer was right. Probably George did need to know. But then again, was this any of their business? A big part of him wished he had simply given her the A. The paper was of publishable quality, after all.

# # #

Years later, there was a time he had one of his students dead to rights only to be informed that the parents were considering a lawsuit. To his great surprise, the new provost informed him, "let them sue. We'll most likely lose. But we'll look good going down." On one occasion, he found two suspicious papers and decided to try an experiment. He went into class the next day and announced, "we've got a problem here. I'm pretty sure there was academic dishonesty on the last assignment. I have decided that if the guilty parties come to my office so we can talk about all of this, I will allow the opportunity to resubmit without penalty." Sure enough, in the next two days, three of his pupils scheduled appointments to confess their sins. The only problem was that neither of the original suspects said a peep.

By the time he had received tenure, Scott had established a protocol for handling these issues. He always included strong language in his course syllabus, highlighting the importance of academic honesty and announcing a policy of referring all cheating cases to the Student Behavior Committee with a recommendation for expulsion. This was mainly bluster on his part. The majority of cases resulted only in an F on the assignment and, hopefully, his having put the fear of God into the little dipshit who had caused the hassle.

Scott had also revised his policy on exams. Early in his career, he had used bluebooks for closed-book, closed-note essay exams. He came to realize, however, that this rewarded those students who were good memorizers and first-draft writers. He decided that take-home essay exams were a more accurate measure of what his students had learned. He didn't want these exams to be a cover for just another term paper, so he asked very specific questions, stipulated a firm word count limit, and reassured them that spelling, grammar, and the other niceties of formal writing would play no factor in the grading. Clarity, however, certainly would.

#

On Thursday morning of finals week, Scott dutifully sat in 108 Brown Hall from eight to ten, the scheduled time of his final exam, while intermittent groups showed up to turn in their exams. At five after ten, he packed up the stack of exams and trundled back to his office, having already decided to use the rest of the day to grade them all and, if he was efficient, also calculate their final grades. Fortified by his third cup of coffee, he was in the middle of a particularly distressing attempt to make sense of the prisoner's dilemma when there was a knock at his office door.

"Professor Greene," Dennis Ridley began. "I overslept. I hope you will accept my final. And I have Jenny Rodrigues's here, too. She got a ride home last night and asked me to turn it in with mine."

"Well, it's eleven fifteen," Scott pretended to sound tough. "That's an hour and fifteen minutes past the deadline. But what the hell? Consider this my Christmas present to you and Jenny. Put them here on the stack."

"Thanks, Professor," Dennis nodded as he exited the office.

Scott smiled to himself, shaking his head at the irresponsibility, and got back to his grading. Twenty minutes or so later, his bullshit detector started to go off. He dug in the pile and retrieved Dennis's and Jenny's exams. Even the most casual glance at their first paragraphs was enough to confirm his worst fears. They were identical, word-for-word. Even the punctuation was the same. "What the fuck?" he uttered aloud. How could they be so stupid? He wasn't all that shocked at Dennis. He was a marginal student at best and probably needed a C+ on the final to pass the course. But Jenny Rodrigues? That was a surprise. She was in the running for an A. Without doing the math, he guessed that a solid B+ would have gotten her over the top. What in the world had she been thinking?

But Scott had other things to worry about right now. There was the rest of his grading, of course.

But he also needed to drive to Watertown and check out the necklace and earrings he had seen. They would be the perfect present for Susan. Well, at least there were two fewer exams requiring his attention. He summarily put big fat red F's on each and returned to the prisoner's dilemma.

\# \# \#

Part of the fun of the quarter system is that you get three do-overs every year. The fall quarter had been okay, but Scott didn't think one of his best. But this quarter! Two of his favorite courses at his preferred times. He was sitting in his office, feeling smug about the introductory lecture he had just delivered, when there was a weak knock at his door. There standing before him was Jenny Rodrigues. "Come in, Jenny," he politely declared. "Please sit down. What can I do for you?"

"Professor Greene," Jenny began, "this is hard for me. But I kind of feel like you lied to me. I came to see you at the very beginning of last quarter."

"Yes, I remember," Scott acknowledged.

"Well, I told you then," Jenny continued, "that I was concerned about taking Ethics from you since I'm very conservative. You told me that my politics and religious beliefs would not matter. All you cared about was understanding and defending a position with strong arguments. But when I got my report card and saw that I had gotten a C-, well, I just don't think that's fair."

This young woman just couldn't be that good of an actress. Scott thought about his reply carefully. "Jenny, you don't have any idea why you received that grade?"

185

"I thought it was because I disagreed with you," she answered. "Was there something else?"

"Yes, I'm afraid there was," Scott was already crafting a plan to undo this mess. "It had to do with the exams that Dennis Ridley turned in for the two of you."

"You mean," Jenny's tone changed to one bordering on outrage, "it's because I left early and didn't turn it in myself?" Scott could see the wheels turning in her head. Yet another inflection change reflected a redirection of her anger. "That's not it, is it? Oh my God. I can't believe he did that."

Scott went into his proper procedure mode. "Just to be sure, please tell me exactly what happened with your exam."

"Let's see," she was clearly trying to remember as accurately as she could, "my cousin called me up and told me she was driving through later that evening and could take me home for Christmas vacation. I was almost done with the exam, anyway. So I just hurried up and finished it. Just before dinner, I knocked on Denny's door. He's just one floor up in our dorm. I asked him to turn it in for me the next day, and he said he would."

"I will see if I can fix all of this," Scott consoled. "But I'm afraid I'll probably have to use your name. Are you okay with that?"

"I guess so," Jenny sounded doubtful.

"Maybe we won't have to," Scott reassured. We'll just have to see. But, in any case, I'll take care of your grade today. I'm glad you came by. Letting that C- stand would have been a tragedy."

# # #

Scott trudged across campus to the registrar's office. The first thing was the grade change. This was easy. Toulmin made it easy for a professor to change a grade they had previously assigned. A simple form, signed and dated, and that was that. Filing a student behavior complaint was a little more complicated. Scott decided to drop into Nancy Dennett's office. She was the assistant registrar and the faculty representative to the Student Behavior Committee. "Hi, Nance, I've got a little problem that I was hoping you could give me some advice with."

"Well, Professor Greene, how nice to see you," she responded with mock formality. "How can I be of service?"

"One of my students from last quarter," Scott began his narrative, "plagiarized his take-home final exam from another student in the class. I gave him an F on the exam and that ensured that he ended up failing the course. The problem is he was going to fail anyway. He put one of the other student in harm's way. I think this is a serious enough case to warrant more than the lousy grade he'd earned in the first place."

"Well," Nancy explained, "you know the drill. Just fill out the disciplinary form. Briefly describe what happened and your suggested remedy. I take it you're going to ask for expulsion. That's the biggie, of course. I will call the student in and interview him. It's his call. He can own up to the cheating and propose an alternate resolution. Or he can dispute the charge and ask for a full hearing with the entire committee."

"What a nightmare," Scott bemoaned. "I can't believe I'm starting the new quarter with this shit."

# # #

Young Mister Ridley's strategy caught everyone off guard. He fully substantiated Jenny Rodrigues's account of the take-home final. But he emphatically denied having copied it. He simply claimed to have no idea of why the two exams were identical. He demanded a full Student Behavior Committee hearing and, at his parents' insistence, the presence of an attorney. The rules for hearings were clear, so the attorney would be there only as an observer. When the Board of Trustees heard about this last development, they insisted that a lawyer for the Board be present as well.

Scott's area of scholarly expertise was the philosophy of law, or what, in law school, would have been called jurisprudence. He had lamented more than once, having not earned a joint J.D. and Ph.D. and trying his hand at being a law professor. If the truth be told, he was a hopeless wannabe lawyer. Now, he had a case to litigate. There were only two witnesses, Scott and Dennis Ridley. Dennis was obviously very nervous but told his narrative with conviction.

"Colleagues and students," Scott began. "Here are two take-home exams," raising them to the committee for effect. "With one or two minor exceptions, they are word-for-word identical, right down to the punctuation. How could this be? Mr. Ridley claims to have no idea. Perhaps it was an amazing coincidence, and both students just happened to express themselves in identical language. Perhaps the explanation is something out of the Twilight Zone, and we just haven't thought of it yet. My account is simple and direct. I contend that Mr. Ridley, having received Jenny's exam the evening before, copied it and simply submitted her work as his own. It pains me, therefore, to point out that Dennis is not only guilty of academic dishonesty but of lying to this committee as well."

The committee's verdict took less than half an hour, but their decision and recommendation to the Dean of Students was confidential until the President issued the college's formal ruling. All of this took a couple of weeks. The committee decreed that Dennis Ridley had indeed cheated. They also recommended Scott's suggested penalty of formal expulsion from Toulmin College. After a lengthy consultation with the Board and its attorney, however, the President chose not to expel him, but to impose a one-year suspension. A decision that Scott had no problems with. Mainly since Dennis and his parents decided not to pursue the matter any further.

# # #

Scott occasionally crossed paths with Dennis in the two years after he returned to complete his baccalaureate. But they had no interaction. The professor was, therefore, dumbfounded when Dennis appeared at his office door the day before graduation. "Professor, I wanted you to know that I'm glad things worked out as they did. I learned a lot of things about myself, and I think I'm a better person because of it." And with that, the two adversaries shook hands.

For nearly a decade, Scott took great satisfaction in the whole sordid affair. He had handled himself honorably and as a professional. He had also saved a young man from a life of dishonesty and perhaps crime. That contentment, however, vanished in the blink of an eye one morning when Scott read in the *New York Times*

that a businessman named Dennis Trevor Ridley
had been formally indicted in one of the largest
Medicare frauds in history. Just to be sure, he
checked his records. Sure enough, the middle name
was the same.

August Full Moon Special

There's a Word For That

John Christopher Nelson

Marty normally took his break at noon, but by 12:23 P.M., he had only just finished the form he'd begun at the start of his shift. Marty spent the next seven minutes with his cursor hovering over the X at the top right corner of the document. If anyone walked by his open office door, he pretended to straighten his already aggressively organized desk.

He was allowed to take his break anytime between noon and 12:30, but could not abide beginning lunch at on odd time. It had to be either the top or the bottom of the hour. Even leaving at a fifteen or forty-five wouldn't work for Marty. Just the thought of it warmed his earlobes and tightened the collar of his shirt.

This was among the inborn qualities that Marty could not avoid, but that left him ever restless.

There were times when the thought of breaking his routine occurred to him, an appealing but risky daydream. A benign idea, but so different from the life that had become normal in its neutrality.

But why normal?

That was never what Marty had aimed for, but it seemed cautious, easy, without the opportunity for misfortune's intrusion. So this was where he found his existence anchored, after years of choosing what he assumed was situationally safe.

At 12:26, he weighed what he should eat today. He usually packed something, thinking it cheaper and healthier. Plus, if he spent the entire hour in his office with the door closed, it afforded him more time to do nothing, to interact with nobody. But some mornings were hectic, and found Marty disinterested in the chore of preparing and carrying a lunch.

The strip malls and shopping centers near his office park didn't offer many appealing options. Miscellaneous fast-food chains, all of them currently offering some new chicken sandwich promotion. Grilled, breaded, spicy, but all somehow the same.

And all of them with pickles, for some godforsaken reason. It would prove to be another of the passing food trends.

There was the Chinese take-out spot that seemed questionable in its quality, no matter the rating proudly Scotch-taped inside the front window. Also, the coffeehouse. He'd purchased a pastry there, more than once. Something light, with berries. Their muffins were always dry.

12:29. Marty decided, without questioning the idea, that he would leave for the rest of the day, instead of returning at 1:30. He'd not make any excuses for himself. None of that quotidian, "I think I ate something bad for lunch," which was an excuse that bothered Marty. If anyone had really eaten something that was off, it would be at least an hour or two before they started feeling ill.

Actually, the incubation period for food poisoning can take up to eight hours.

"My kids," fill-in-the-blank, also would not work, because Marty had none of his own. Marty was not married or seeing anyone regularly, so he couldn't even say that Samantha or Rhonda or whoever had just discovered she was with child, let alone going into labor. Even that wouldn't have worked, because Marty was an openly gay man. Sam or Ronald or whoever also would not be calling Marty to inform him they were carrying his baby.

Marty's job was nothing incredible. Even in a management position, he was not particularly proud of his career, albeit unashamed of it. He never saved lives at work, but he also did not clean toilets or pick up trash with his bare hands. Nothing the matter with those jobs, but Marty was a few tics south of mysophobia.

It's a give and take.

Decades ago, Marty had started as a runner for the office when he was an undergrad. It was a paid internship and, in time, he applied to a position in the human resources department. Now, secure in his management role, his life was the dullest, yet most pleasant, it had ever been. When people asked, after he'd already told them his job title, what exactly it was that he did, he often found himself grasping for a concrete description of duties.

What is it I do? What is it to do?

There were documents that appeared on his desk, and often the attached name was one he'd never seen before. Sometimes it was a name with which he'd grown too familiar, annoyed or amused by its reappearance in turn. He wondered how many of the names and faces in this building he could actually match. Mostly employees who were either very good or very bad at their position.

Probably somewhere in the neighborhood of twelve percent.

Marty reviewed HR documents, and if he felt there were changes to be made, he'd send the document back with suggestions. Sometimes the indicated changes would be made without remark, the document would return to his inbox, and he would forward it to the person who was intended to receive it. There was once or twice that the document came back to him without changes, but with an explanation of why the changes had not been made. The few times this happened, Marty seconded the reasoning and forwarded the document down the line. Marty seldom knew on whose desk these documents would terminally arrive and what would be done with them at that point. But he didn't care. He'd checked his box in the chain of command.

There were days when it slipped his mind what kind of company he worked for. Some longish, legalese-heavy description of an abstract necessity. Marty sometimes thought on this when he wasn't engaged with anything more important. This was often the case.

Marty struggled more each day with assigning importance. The concept grew increasingly amorphous for him, with each passing year.

That's how capitalism functions. Everyone sells something, even if it's an intangible something. It's never any less odd to live in a society where it's possible to exchange money for an idea.

Marty put his things in his briefcase and powered down his desktop. It was 12:34, he had already clocked out four minutes earlier, and he would not be returning. He was certain of it. He would make no mention of his spontaneous decision when he left the office. Instead, he locked his door behind him and walked down the hall, issuing smiles or small waves where appropriate.

Taylor, a newer intern, effervesced a twee, "Hi, Marty," and his response was deliberately subdued. As they passed each other, heading in opposite directions, she asked where he was off to and, without stopping, he told her he was going to the beach. He wasn't, and she must not have known how to react, because she said nothing else. Maybe she felt indifferent about his destination.

Most people who work in offices have learned to be adept at small talk without actually caring in the slightest about the topic of discussion. Taylor might not have even caught the word "beach."

Marty sometimes fantasized about having a more melodramatic life than the one he schlepped through. It was nothing special or exciting, but it was also not dreary or lonely. Marty did have friends outside of work and went on dates as often as he cared too, which wasn't very. Still, films and books he'd seen and read made him think that it'd be somehow romantic if he left work for good and went home to hang himself or cut his wrists in the bathtub like that guy from the painting or the other guy from the second *Godfather*.

Wait, not romantic. Tragic.

Maybe both, depending on his reason, whether he left a note, what the note would tell the people who read it.

Who would find it and read it first?

Probably his landlord or a police officer.

How dull. Wait. Was the guy from that painting in a bathtub?

If he went with the tub route, he'd have to pick something appropriate to play on the small radio perched atop the medicine cabinet. But that wouldn't work either, because whatever he'd been playing would have ended by the time anyone discovered him. It would take a moment before anyone would think to call in a wellness check. And by then, whatever was playing could be embarrassing and out of character.

Marty possessed no self-loathing and he'd never considered suicide, but was always fascinated by the way in which popular culture characterized the act as somehow poetic. But also, Marty's understanding of what it meant for something to be poetic reached about as far as his understanding of irony, which was not a generous length. Vague ideas, not interpreted inaccurately, but also missing the point on an emotional dartboard.

For reasons he couldn't articulate, if he pretended he was walking down the street with the intention of self-harm, it made him feel like so much more of a real human, and it threaded each of his actions with greater depth. Why, this could be the last time Marty would ever take in the sounds and smells of the city as he carried his briefcase along its sidewalks. It didn't even matter that one of the case's locks stuck. He wouldn't need it anymore.

But there was nothing especially beautiful about anything he was hearing or smelling. He thought a moment longer and changed his mind. It wasn't beautiful or tragic.

It's depressing.

That was the word, and it had nothing to do with poetry. This conclusion discomposed Marty, and he realized this might also have been because he hadn't ingested anything but coffee so far today.

It made no sense to him, really. He'd leave these musings about suicide alone.

Why waste so much thought on something I won't do?

Before outpacing them, he glanced at a mother pushing her daughter in a stroller. The little girl had memories of a meal smeared around her lips and cheeks, fingers viscid where she'd touched the food. She appeared fully content to be this mess of a toddler. This little girl, now out of sight as Marty continued to think about her, held no concept of herself as a person, no grasp of self-identity, and yet was happy to be alive, even if unsuitably presentable for public display.

What is it to experience something without knowing what it was? Is happiness more pure before you know how it is supposed to feel? Maybe that's why children always look like that.

Maybe putting a name to a feeling distilled it and assigned it some meaning of elevated significance. Or perhaps something is robbed from an emotion once it's named. Maybe this acted as a sort of limiter on a concept. Where once, childhood possibilities of happiness were boundless, now they were kept within a constraint, like everything else. This must be how children are conditioned to accept society, to surrender to the rigidity of its boundaries. A series of boxes, placed within larger boxes.

Matryoshka dolls for acceptable etiquette.

He wished he could remember more from his own, now distant, childhood. But then life might seem as though it were lacking something profound and indiscernible. Better to focus on the pleasures that are allowed to adults. Taxes, television reruns, decorating one's desk at the office, dispiriting dates, underwhelming intimacy, wine—but only ever red—reading best sellers, abandoning best sellers, purchasing new patio chairs, washing the chair cushions again because they still smell like The Home Depot, refilling ice trays, waiting on hold with the electric company, completing crosswords, not fully grasping Wordle—a few years prior, Sudoku had also proven elusive—trying to remember how to change a tire, trying something different at the coffeehouse, wishing to have ordered the usual instead, picking up the best seller again and subsequently regretting it again, commiserating with friends about the stark difference between the cost of movie tickets now and thirty years ago, flipping the calendar to a new month, refilling the Brita pitcher but slouching on replacing the filter, adding paper towels to the grocery list, forgetting the grocery list before heading to the store, farmers' markets, neglecting to use fresh produce before it wilts, assessing the smell of milk after its best-by date, scooping the cat box, adjusting the temperature on the water heater, starting to watch the evening news, but turning it off less than five minutes later, because no matter what it is, it's always only more of the same, never knowing which knife to use for which cheese at a dinner party, addressing cards for the holidays and realizing the postage stamps have run out, wishing there was enough room on the patio to grow something to sell at a farmers' market, thinking about the beach, but not actually visiting the ocean.

Nothing so bad about all of that.

Marty was still deciding what he should do. It's not often that a person takes their whole day off without telling anyone. Marty would be a fool to waste it.

He paused at a bus stop and folded his cardigan as neatly as possible so he could stuff it inside his briefcase. The day was already much warmer than it had been on his way to work. Soon enough, it would be 1:30, and Marty realized he might be hearing from work shortly after that. He supposed they'd be concerned or bothered. In either case, he decided to let them feel however it was they were going to feel and that he would rather he not have to hear about it. He silenced his phone and locked it in his briefcase, where he wouldn't misplace it.

Maybe it will get stuck in there.

Maybe Taylor had been listening when he told her he was going to the beach and, perhaps when it was clear he was not coming back, she would tell their coworkers what he had said. She seemed too kind and private to go out of her way to tell on him, but she also struck Marty as honest.

He hoped that they would all silently congratulate him, as he was now congratulating himself. Marty deserved a day off at the beach, even if this was a fictional version of what he was going to do with his afternoon.

A fictional day at a fictional beach, he smiled.

Marty did not look at the route number on the front of the bus, and did not speak to the bus driver. He boarded, paid his fare, and took a seat at the rear of the vehicle, with his worn briefcase on his lap.

Not long after the bus pulled away from the curb, it passed the mother with the stroller. Marty was again amused by the slovenly, carefree child, also being chauffeured to a destination she did not know or care about.

The Truth About Selfishness

Michael Eyre

Our genes are selfish, science says,
they're always wanting their own way.
But selfishness is bad, we're taught.
A gaping divide one could say.

Should you always self-sacrifice?
Let other people's needs usurp.
Keep taking bullets for someone
who moans your blood messes up their shirt.

Or should you act from pure self-love
to ensure 'me' is self-preserved?
Just take, take, take all that you can.
Go grab your prize like it's deserved.

In truth selfishness is best shared.
Give that prize to those you cherish.
Share the joy it brings with the world.
Go on, be absolutely selfish!

Runner's Epitaph

Michael Eyre

When a runner dies
have not a care for
their bank balance size.

Their preeminent
qualification,
or immense mansion.

The fancy title
that came with their job,
or scale of their pay.

Just remember their
personal best times
for 5 and 10k!

August New Moon Special

Bigfoot

Peter Cashorali

You're driving in the mountains with the top down, an ornately engraved shotgun on the seat next to you. Bigfoot climbs up onto the road, even in sunlight just a silhouette but his big bristly body unmistakable for anything else. You reach for the shotgun and fire at him. He lurches away. You keep driving. This wasn't a good idea. You haven't even wounded him, merely been rude. He'll travel down the slopes and show up at another bend in the road, resentful now, rejected, whatever his original reason for approaching you colored by displeasure. And he isn't Bigfoot.

the stories of chris

Blake Edwards

Chris Kerny arrived on the campus of Cypress Academy without pomp or circumstance. It was the beginning of junior year, his second, my first. There was no envoy of black SUV's like the ones that carried the children of celebrities, no collegiate coaches carefully protecting him from injury as if he were a star recruit destined for professional athletics, no dollies filled to the brim with designer luggage like the ones that arrived for the fashion forward foreign heiresses. He was just some guy. He used to tell this story about how, on that first move in day junior year, after his parents left, he smoked a blunt out in the open next to the practice football field. According to Chris, the dean of student affairs was walking his dog right by the field at the same time and caught him with smoke coming out of his ears. As the story goes, the dean showed Chris mercy that day because it was his first day in a new environment, and decided they could keep the incident between themselves, so long as Chris now understood the rules of aforementioned new environment. Chris agreed, and promised that that would be his last blunt until he was back in his bedroom in Cambridge. It was not. I always told Chris he should be a writer, he always refused, for reasons I do not immediately remember. I do wish he had taken my advice though, he told these stories much better than I do.

My first inclination as to Chris' cause of death was wrong, slightly. I had suspected overdose. Delany Smith, originally from Beverly

Hills, was the first to let me know that he had died, but she did not know the details, so I hung up on her in search of the truth. I went to social media. The outpouring of tributary messages that he would never see was just beginning, but the only post with some information was a screenshot of a news article posted by Veronica Hampstead. I fucked Veronica back during junior year, took her virginity actually. She was a porky number, with a thick Boston accent and collegiate hockey aspirations; it was not my proudest orgasm. Chris teased me for that conquest endlessly, but I think he would have fucked Veronica too, given the opportunity. From her screenshot I found the full article, and sat up in bed as I read the harrowing details of my friend's murder.

It had just happened early in the morning the day before. He was home from the University of Vermont on Thanksgiving break. As my semester trudged on, I wondered silently why their break was so long, goddamn. He was hanging out with one of his public school friends, they had gotten a bottle of vodka. Sounded just like Chris. He used to fill empty water bottles up with vodka and sip them in class until he was forced to excuse himself to the bathroom and vomit. I knew I was reading the correct article. Naturally, after buying the bottle, he contacted a drug dealer in pursuit of prescription pills. Undoubtedly Xanax, his drug of choice. Back in school he would return home every weekend, and every Sunday night he came back to school bearing "xans". Every Friday afternoon I would ask him to bring some back for me, offering to pay a premium, and every Monday morning he would tell me that he totally had brought some back for me, but, unfortunately, he had taken them all the night before, immediately upon return to campus. It didn't matter how many there were. "It's a compulsion," he would tell me, and I would laugh it off, thinking only about the drugs I didn't have. They met up with the drug dealer at a local park, the public school friend stayed behind the park's fence as Chris completed the transaction. Allegedly, in a drunken stupor, Chris smashed the bottle of vodka and bum rushed the drug dealer with a shard of broken glass as a weapon. The drug dealer, armed with a real knife, fought his attacker's advances until he stood victorious, stained by another man's blood. I imagine it happened something like a great bull fight: my pale, portly friend, red faced, angrily charging at this matador of a drug dealer while the dealer strategically stabbed him nine times in the face, neck, and upper chest until the mighty, mighty bull keeled over in defeat.

I don't remember when exactly I met Chris Kerny, but it had to have been early on junior year because by the turn of the seasons we were hanging out almost everyday. We would lift weights together, and then, back at the dorm, he would offer me a lip-full of chewing tobacco if I agreed to shower in the stall next to his. We showered with nothing but the thin tile wall between our wet, naked, teenage bodies, and we talked about everything we could think of while we spat brown slugs of tobacco tinted saliva down the drains at our feet. We talked about the Red Sox, what girls we wanted to fuck, what music we liked to listen to. We didn't hangout much outside of those weekday workouts and showers. One day, while hanging out

206

with Chris after a shower, I was jonesing for a cigarette— badly. Chris was feeling the same.

"You know who definitely has cigarettes?" He asked rhetorically while laying on the floor of the dorm room he shared with the son of a Mexican horse breeder. "Tom. We should go up to his room and steal his cigarettes! I think I saw where he hides his pack last time I was in his room." Tom was a goofball. A rich, midwestern, dimwit that everyone took advantage of. My addiction got the better of me, I agreed. We devised a plan where I lured Tom out of his room while Chris snuck in and stole the cigarettes. The plan succeeded. Back in Chris' room we lit up one cigarette apiece and smoked them away in silence. After we finished, Chris spoke up again, more seriously than I had ever heard him speak before, "I think we should give Tom his cigarettes back. I saw small round burn marks on his arms the other day. I think he needs these a lot more than we do." A wave of relief washed over my body, I'd noticed the burn marks too. Once again, I lured Tom out of his room and once again Chris snuck in, only this time it was to return what we had stolen. I was glad that Chris had the courage to speak up in that moment when I didn't. The courage to call out the error of our ways and seek to rectify it. He was right. Tom needed those cigarettes infinitely more than we did. Chris understood pain much better than me.

That first trimester of junior year at Cypress was pure anarchy. Walking on our campus was like walking through a reanimated cemetery on Halloween night while the braindead zombies of grotesquely privileged teenagers traversed the manufactured paths and greeneries. It all started the year before; a year that was marked by a litany of offenses ranging from burglary to child pornography to non-lethal overdose. The following summer, a task force was assembled to attempt to figure out how to curb the destructive urges of a student body that was as wealthy, savvy, and well connected as any group of teenagers in the world. The task force decided that if the students had less free time, there would be less time for them to get into trouble. Weekend leave requests would now run through encrypted online servers so that signatures could not be forged, the usual mandatory weekday study hall now extended to Friday nights as well, and a half day of Saturday school was implemented. To a student body that had grown accustomed to a four-and-half day school week, the new schedule was sacrilege. Their plan failed miserably. It took us a few weeks to adjust, but by the end of September descent into debauchery had begun. Students were auctioning off their prescription medications to the highest bidder, freshmen girls were devising secret routes to continue sneaking into the rooms of seniors and post graduates, and parents were smuggling their children contraband during clandestine meetings at local restaurants. On top of that, due to the swift and drastic changes in school policies, enrollment applications dropped by almost seventy five percent, threatening the size of the student body, and the schools ability to operate. In disgrace, our headmaster was forced to resign, effective at the end of the trimester, and the new policies would be reversed going forward. The students had won, and we planned to celebrate that win at our winter celebration, the headmaster's last formal event.

In the week leading up to the winter celebration it was understood that all the cool kids would be taking Xanax shortly before the start of the event. The winter celebration happened on the last Friday night before winter finals week every year, and it was known as the formal close of the first trimester. All students and faculty were required to dress in their most formal attire, sit in the chapel for speeches and formal performances by the school band, and then shuffle in the cold to the dining hall for a formal dinner with a randomized seating chart so that everyone could be uncomfortable and eat bad food with people they would never normally speak to. It was a fucking snooze fest.

I was on Xanax heavily at the time, back then everyone was. I was sleeping under my desk in class, nodding off with food still in my mouth at the dining hall, and stumbling around campus at night begging anybody who would talk to me for even half a pill. It felt like all the other students were doing similar things. At the winter celebration it was amplified to near comic proportions. I don't remember much from the event, proof that the Xanax was working, but I do remember Lilith Foust getting expelled for dancing intoxicatedly on top of a table at the dinner. I'm sure that the rest of the ceremony's events were just as amusing. I don't have a solid memory of the events that transpired that night after the celebration had concluded either, but those events have been recanted to me so many times that I should be able to piece the story together somewhat reliably:

I fumbled my way into the dorm blacked on out Xanax about thirty minutes before lights out

while all the other boys were peeling off their
jackets and ties. I saw Chris, and he told me that he
had a blunt he'd be willing to share with me as long
as we smoked it in my room because his roommate
would not allow it in theirs. I had a single. Smoking
weed indoors at boarding school is certain death
unless adhering to the proper precautions, but in my
inebriated state I'd forgotten to secure the necessary
safeguards. I had opened the window, but there was
no fan running to thin out the smoke, no towel
under the door to stop the smoke from spreading,
and no scented spray on hand to mitigate the odor.
We finished the blunt quickly, but my room stunk
of weed nonetheless, as did the entirety of the third
floor hallway that housed both my room and his.
Lights out had not yet happened, which meant that
the dorm mother, the teacher that lived in an
apartment in the dorm and was responsible for our
general well being, would still be coming around
room to room for her nightly check. Chris retreated
to his room while I, with the last active braincell in
my head, decided to take a shower to at least get the
stench of marijuana off my body. I returned from
the shower nearly asleep before I even dried off. I
climbed onto my sheetless bed in just a towel, the
combination of Xanax and weed ravishing my still-
developing body, making it impossible to keep my
eyes open. As I nodded off, a few of my senior
friends, the elder statesmen of the dorm, banded
together and, out of the goodness of their hearts,
decided to save my ass. One of them sprayed my
room down with cologne until it no longer reeked.
One of them sprayed down the hallway to obfuscate
the source of the stench. One of them lied to the
dorm mother when she asked him if he smelled

what she was smelling. I am grateful to this day that I had people that cared enough about me to look out for me. Chris was not so lucky. He hadn't showered, and the dorm mother traced the smell back to his room. He was given the standard punishment: a five day out of school suspension, seen as a vacation to him, but not to his parents. I still remember the guilt I felt when I found out Chris got in trouble. It seemed so unfair. Sure, I had more self awareness and a better support system but still, we were doing the exact same things at the exact same time. It wasn't fair that he was gone but I'm still here.

As soon as I finished the article I knew I wanted to attend Chris' funeral. I did some digging and found out that there would be a service and reception the following Wednesday, the day before Thanksgiving. Today was Thursday, my last day of classes before break. I would take the bus from my upstate New York campus into Boston, spend the night a friend's apartment, go home sometime on Saturday, then return to Boston on Wednesday for the funeral. Boston is only about thirty minutes from my family's home. For now though, I was still in my college apartment, and I was going out that night. I took a shower before I left, and thought back to the showers I'd shared with Chris. I began to sob in the shower, and continued to sob while I washed up and returned to my bedroom. I found a notebook, sat naked on my bedroom floor, and sobbed while I wrote a poem about Chris. It was raw and emotional and terrible. I haven't looked at it since. I wiped my tears, finished getting dressed, and left for my night out. I arrived at my then best friend, now wife's, apartment, and her roommate greeted me with the playful rudeness that defined our relationship.

"Why are your eyes so red?" She asked, expecting me to retort with a quip about the copious amount of weed I smoked prior to my arrival.

"I was just crying," I snapped back impatiently with all the honesty and energy I could muster. My best friend, already abreast of the situation at hand, shoved a drink in my hand in an attempt to lighten the mood. I remained quiet, pensive, introverted— not totally uncommon for a night out with her friends. The next morning I was back at my apartment with my girlfriend, and she was helping me pack so that I would not miss my bus. Right before I was about to leave she stood between me and the bedroom door, asking me to have sex with her one last time before we left for break. She threw her petite body against the door, pulled her panties to the side, and begged me to take her from behind. Wearily I agreed, despite my lack of interest, like a dutiful boyfriend should. I tried my hardest, but it was not hard enough.

I could feel the insecurity in the air as I tucked myself back into my pants. "You're just sad about your friend, right baby?"

"Yeah, I'm just really stressed right now," I said, but that was half a lie. Truthfully I hated her, but I did not realize I hated her for another three months or so.

I didn't hangout with Chris very much for the rest of junior year after he got back from his suspension. I'm not sure why. I hung out with my friends, he hung out by himself and went home on the weekends. I had an uneventful summer, working four days a week as an urban farmer and still hopelessly clinging to my dream of playing college basketball. I arrived back on the Cypress Academy campus as a senior, and one of the lucky students chosen to be housed in one of the two new dormitories on campus. They were for upperclassmen only, with fifty single rooms each, one for boys and one for girls. Chris was in the new dorm too, I was on the third floor, he was on the first. With the money I saved from urban farming I invested in my first electronic weed pen so that I could get high discreetly on demand.

Once word got out that I was getting my own weed I started seeing a lot more of Chris. My older friends had graduated by then and I preferred being alone at that time. However, I welcomed Chris whenever he knocked on my door. He would sit in my beanbag chair while I lay in the bed and we would talk, laugh, and tell stories while he waited for me to inevitably pass him the weed or a cigarette. I could tell that he was using me to achieve his daily fixes, but I didn't mind. By Chris, being used was a pleasure. I appreciated the company, and I thought Chris' stories were very entertaining. Plus, it was my way of assuaging the previous year's guilt. He visited my room whenever he needed to; early in the morning before I had showered, during the day on breaks from his classes, late at night while I was dressed in only underwear, and I would let him. He tried to repay me anyway he could. He offered companionship, would do favors for me when I asked, and shared his contraband whenever he had any to share. Never Xanax though, those were always all for him.

I quit playing basketball early on during senior year to have more time for doing drugs, and eventually my room became a hangout not just for Chris, but for a full group of wayward boys who all needed some kind of substantive fix. There was Hank Kramer, born in Guatemala and adopted by well-to-do Massachusetts parents; Evan Cash, a new money douchebag whose last name was the happiest coincidence in the world in his own opinion; Jake Bradly, a virgin in the grade below us; Nate Briggs, a recruited lacrosse player with a foot fetish; and Ernie Urlacher, from Alaska. They were not my best friends, but they were a like-minded and fun cohort; I enjoyed their company greatly. We laughed, we danced, we debated, we fought; we acted like schoolboys on the precipice of becoming men. It was those kinds of random connections that made boarding school bearable. To us it was not novel, or prestigious, or extravagant— it was just high school, and high school sucks.

We all had English class together, we usually got high beforehand. It was taught by a first year teacher, Ms. Hathaway, and the only students in the class were my ragtag crew of raucous stoners, a few other misfit boys that stood firmly on the periphery of our group, and two girls who could spit and swear worse than any of the boys when properly inspired— one from Maine, one from Indonesia. With eyes glazed over we spent the year tormenting our rookie teacher endlessly, making sure that, come summertime, she had earned her place in the program. Lessons were disrupted, assignments were bullshitted, and mandatory reading was rarely ever completed. We made a glorious mockery of the elite education out parents paid exorbitantly to expose us to. There was a presentation due on the last day of school; Chris was scheduled to present last. He stood in front of the class and presented exactly one slide before returning to his seat.

"That's it?" I called out in a bit of jestful heckling.

"It's my last day of high school ever," he answered, dead pan, before sitting back down in his chair. He was right. High school was over, the real world was on the horizon, and he could not have cared less.

After the bus ride from Ithaca to Boston I texted my parents from my friend's apartment to let them know I would be attending a funeral over this break, attempting to avoid any awkward conversations happening in person. My attempt failed. At brunch with my mother the day before the funeral she told me she read the news in an email blast sent out by Cypress Academy. We spoke on Chris for a while. She said that she could not imagine the turmoil I must presently be going through. She said it was odd that we would all continue living while he was doomed to exist as a twenty year-old eternally. I agreed. Then she mentioned the fact that my younger brother was also named Chris. I'd forgotten until right then. Their legal names were different, but Chris is a nickname they shared. The connection is faint, but it is there. I pondered this connection in search of meaning for years after my mother's comment, but ultimately decided there is none. Sometimes the strings that bind us humans together are so whisper thin that they bear no meaning at all.

I had a brief conversation with my dad on the morning of the funeral. Back then all of our conversations were brief. I wore a white shirt, navy jacket, blue tie, khaki pants, and navy boat shoes. "We have to get you a nice suit. It's time you got a nice full suit," he said as he sat on the edge of his bed in a wife-beater and boxer-briefs. I agreed. "I read that article about your friend. Does that sound like something he would have gotten himself into?" I answered truthfully. "Well then," he said, letting his voice trail off in order to convey a message that I understood: we are all solely responsible for our own actions. Probably a relic from his stint in rehab. I wouldn't know, I've never been. Our conversation was over after that.

Evan Cash picked me up for the funeral. Jake Bradly was with him, he'd flown in from North Carolina the night before to stay at Evan's New Hampshire home for the funeral, then fly home for Thanksgiving after the service. I climbed into the burgundy leather seats of Cash's all black Mercedes Benz, and was greeted by the boys, now young men, I hadn't seen since graduation. Cash tossed a bag of weed at me and asked me to roll it into joints. I didn't know what the joints were for, but I had no qualms about the task I'd been assigned. I'd spent the majority of the previous summer living out of a drug den in Boston, I was the designated joint roller. I have a gift for rolling picturesque joints; a gift I would share with fiends, drug dealers, local rappers, and any other stone that rolled through the abandoned property, in exchange for free drugs and alcohol. It was a great deal for a spoiled teenager that wanted for nothing besides a cheap high.

The funeral was held at one of the chapels on the campus of Boston College, we were early. The football team was practicing nearby, we heard their testosterone fueled roars as we exited the vehicle. Evan and Jake led the way while I followed behind, taking in the scenery. It was late November in New England: the sky was a gloomy hue of navy-grey, the trees were bare, save for a few burnt orange leaves that refused to die, the air was brittle yet sharp. As we approached the chapel I began to make out the sullen faces of fellow funeral goers. Evan and Jake navigated around the crowd and through a thin forest until we emerged on the other side, in front of a small pond. I was confused until Evan pulled out one of the joints I'd rolled in the car. I objected, referencing a piece of advice given to me by Chris himself.

It was the morning of graduation and we were in the hallway of one of the school buildings preparing for the procession. I was nursing a wicked hangover, but had still mustered up the strength to smoke a little weed. I asked Chris if he'd done the same. "No," he answered, to my surprise. "There are some times in life where you wanna be present."

Those words echoed in my heart as I tried, completely against my nature, to pressure my friends against smoking weed. I recited the words, arguing that if there was ever a time where Chris would have thought it best to be present and sober, surely it would be at his own funeral. They argued back, claiming that we were honoring his memory by partaking in one of his favorite pastimes in preparation for his send off. So there we were: three stooges trying to interpret the opinions of a dead man with a pond in front of us, a football team to our right, weed still burning, and a funeral threatening to start at any moment. Eventually, they talked me into it. I still don't know why I abandoned my principles so easily. I gave in despite never feeling good about what we were doing. I told myself that it was okay because it was the first, and only, reunion of our English class gang that we would ever have with Chris above ground, but I knew in my soul that smoking right then was wrong. Evan sparked the joint but the wind whipped ferociously, another classic characteristic of late fall in New England, causing the joint to smoke unevenly and poorly. Maybe it was Chris stepping in, confirming his wishes, and once again giving me support when I lacked courage. Maybe it was just the fucking wind. All I know is I didn't get high.

When we returned from the forest the crowd outside the chapel had grown significantly. It was mostly older people whom I suspected to be family members. I didn't notice a lot of younger people who may have been Chris' public school friends. After a minute, on the edge of the crowd, I spotted some familiar faces. It was a few of the boys from the outskirts of our English class, along with Allie Ostertag. Allie had been Nate Brigg's girlfriend throughout high school, and Nate and Chris were best friends, so the three of them had been somewhat of a trio back then. Her and Nate had since broken up, but I thought it a nice gesture of her to fly in from Berlin anyway. Evan, Jake, Allie, and the few other boys from English class were the only people I recognized at Chris' funeral. In the aftermath, my mother considered it disgraceful that Cypress Academy didn't send a representative to mourn the tragic loss of a recent graduate, but I assured her that he would not have wanted any

representative there to mourn on the academy's
behalf.

The best part of Catholicism is the aesthetic.
Grandiose gothic architecture, colorful stained glass
windows, artwork that reflects obsessively solemn
and dutiful devotion. A vibrant stained glass
window pane captured my attention as the crowd
was shuffled into the chapel. I took my seat in a
pew in one of the middle rows. Once everyone had
settled in, the casket, closed, was walked down the
aisle and placed in front of the alter for all to see.
The funeral started with a hymn. Then some word
from the parish priest. He told the one about how
God sometimes calls troubled people home early
because their souls are too pure for our world. Then
the two eulogies: one from each of his older sisters.
I listened intently to the stories of their chubby
blond brother running around the house as a young
rascal, but with every pause in their speech I would
be distracted by the weeping coming diagonally
across the aisle. Finally, my curiosity got the better
of me and I looked over to the source of the
weeping. It was Chris' grandmother, weeping at the
sight of her grandson's closed casket. I did not look
over again.

In that box was a friend of mine, with nine
stab wounds, who would never walk the earth
again. He would never again be rejected by a girl;
or cut a song off after thirty seconds, even if he
liked it, due to lack of attention span; or dance like
an idiot while his pants sagged halfway off his ass.
Chris' story was over while the stories of his friends
and family members were forced to continue
without one of their most integral characters.
Everyone stood up as the casket was marched back

down the aisle and out the door. The family followed first, the rest of the attendees, myself included, followed behind shortly after. The funeral was over.

The family ducked away into an envoy of vehicles, lead by the hearse, on their way to the private burial. My former Cypress classmates and I lingered outside the chapel for a moment, enjoying cigarettes. There was a reception at an Italian restaurant in the North End, most of the guests would be attending. The few stray boys from English class had decided against going to the reception, so Jake, Allie, Evan, and I piled into Evan's car and drove to the restaurant. We smoked one of the joints I rolled on the way. I puffed with a clear conscience, my respectful abstinence was over. With red eyes, we entered the reception. There were hors d'oeuvres. Some people from the funeral that I didn't know tried to make small talk with me in line for the buffet. People never consider the different kinds of folks from different areas of their life that will be forced to mingle at their funeral. I exited each conversation at the first given opportunity.

I took a seat at a square table with my boarding school chums. We gossiped about all the things that extremely economically advantaged teenagers gossip about: who wintered in Zurich, who recently received botched plastic surgery, who was in rehab. Allie shared with us that, during his friendship with Chris and the tail end of their relationship, Nate had become addicted to Xanax too. He was being treated at a rehab facility in California. That's why he was unable to attend the funeral. It was the kind of rehab facility that cuts off all contact with the outside world, so she didn't even know if Nate knew Chris was dead. Nate still calls me from time to time asking for Xanax, all these years later. Chris' other best friend, Hank, also lacking direction, had joined the military. He was stationed in Iraq. Chris had been laid to rest with neither of his best friends able to say goodbye. Near the exit, Chris' family had set up large poster boards decorated with photos of him throughout his life. The pictures started from birth, and contained images from parts of Chris' life that I didn't even know existed. For some reason, I used my cellphone camera to take a picture of the board that displayed Chris in middle childhood; before disappointment, before drugs, before life stuffed him into an early grave. I wanted to remember him that way. A way in which I had never known him.

We left the funeral reception in search of real food. There was a sushi restaurant downtown that I'd been wanting to try. We smoked another joint on the way. We arrived at the restaurant, sat down at a table, and ordered the most expensive thing on menu: the sushi boat to share, plus individual options for each of us. The boat came out quickly. We talked again as we ate, aloofly ignoring the horrific circumstances that brought us all together. It was as if we were just four old friends having a casual reunion. That's when I noticed the privileged carelessness that we all traipsed through the world with. We float through life free of any real challenge or consequence; using money, privilege, and status as justification for why we should be allowed to galavant chaotically across the globe without giving a damn about what we damage. We break things and wait for other people

to fix them so often that we forget some things
cannot be put back together and made whole again.
We do whatever we want, all the time, without
caring who it hurts, even if the victim is ourselves.
It's a despicable way of living, but it's the only life
I've ever known, and the only one I'll ever have to.
We stuffed our gluttonous faces until we were near
illness, split the bill across four of our parents credit
cards, and left to continue our lives. I claimed the
leftover sushi.

Perseveration
Larena Nellies-Ortiz

Temple Street

RJ Bee

Ray stumbles out onto the sidewalk. He tries to squint, but the sun is too bright. He takes a deep breath and lets it flow through him.

His phone confirms the time: 4:45pm. It's that lost time of day, when it's too late to start over, but too early to give up and go to sleep. He's had so many of those days recently, but almost all of them were him, alone, in his empty house. Today was a nice change, to feel an open, unpredictable afternoon, especially after the last year. Ray left the conference at lunchtime with a few others, one thing led to another, and now he's drunk on the streets of Boston.

The conference was a good distraction. He'd be a modern day Marco Polo, bringing insights from the new world to his office in Santa Fe: Everything is going to be on the blockchain. The people he met and drank with this afternoon gave him a sense of conviviality. He felt welcomed, like he belonged. He left the bar last, after having one more by himself, and now he was buoyant with socialization and beer.

He heads down Commonwealth, walking through the wide park bisecting the street, a secret garden. He passes a pair of lovers gazing into each other's eyes. He thinks about walking up and putting his hand between their faces to see if they notice. He doesn't think they would. How beautiful, he thinks, to be in carefree love.

On the walk, he commits to a plan—walk to the hotel, eat dinner, take a shower, go to bed, head back home in the morning. Keep it simple, that's what his friends keep telling him. He lived in Boston a lifetime ago, but his life here feels theoretical, fragments of something, not a material truth. Pieces of it tug at him, but he shrugs them off as he walks.

He remembers the first restaurant he and his wife visited in the city, an Italian joint in the North End. Clams with red sauce, veal, risotto. Overpriced and touristy, but novel. Life was full of novelty then—young people in a new city, making a new life. This was before everything that's now wreaking havoc on him.

He walks past the State House, and is smacked with a feeling of deja vu. Shreds of detail swirl around him—the golden dome of the capitol, kissing his wife's thin lips, her dark hair tickling his face, the river shimmering in the distance. He's perplexed—is this one memory, or an amalgam of various things from his life with her?

When he booked this trip, he wanted to get away. He realizes now that he didn't get away at all. His life followed him here, as it follows him everywhere. It was naive of him to have expected this trip to be devoid of these memories, formative in their relationship. He realizes then, standing on that corner, that their first apartment together is just around the corner.

A minute later, he's at the top of Temple Street, gazing down the block, like looking at a geometric painting—shadows at a 45-degree angle, cutting across and casting perfect half-darkness on all the buildings.

As he walks down Temple, the lit half of the apartment buildings give off an intense, fire-like hue. He can't remember his address, but he knows they lived in apartment 2. Struck by a sudden sense of longing, he's torn.

He could turn around, go back to the hotel, and not dive into this murky lake of memories. He could continue to push his feelings down, continue to walk away from it all. He thinks, at the same time, that if he could just see his old apartment, he could get some closure, and start to pacify the raging storm inside of him.

Ray prowls to the end of the block and back, pacing the sidewalk like a drunk lion, hot and burning with indecision. He has another recollection, of himself and his wife coming home from a bar, late at night. He had walked up to the wrong building, trying to fit his key in the door.

His wife was laughing. "You idiot," she said, trying to catch her breath.

All he could manage was, "They all look the same!"

Now, he looks up at the buildings and smiles.

His body is moving, and he's on the stoop of one of a building in the middle of the block, pressing the buzzer for apartment 2.

A voice says, with real curiosity, "Hello?"

"Uh, hi. My name is Ray. I think I used to live here. In your apartment? A long time ago, like 15 years ago."

She says, "Come on up." He walks into the lobby, and sees the familiar red wine colored carpet and the banister of dark carved wood, worn smooth by thousands of human palms. He has an instant kinship with the building, remembering himself walking upstairs like these countless times.

As his hand glides along the banister, he remembers the last meal he had with his wife, at the tapas place. He thinks about how her bare elbow balanced on the smooth curvature of the bar. He knocks on the door to apartment 2. It opens a crack, and he sees a small woman looking at him. She has glasses and dark hair, her face is wrinkled like a raisin.

"I'm sorry to bother," he says. "I just wanted to see the apartment? I used to live here."

She looks at him, and then says over her shoulder, "He says he used to live here." She looks back at him. "Come on in."

He walks into an apartment that seems like it's been lived in for centuries. It's the home of a couple—a pair of men's black loafers next to his feet, and two coats and a hat on a rack. Gazing to his left, he sees the kitchen, which has a table set with two glasses, two plates, and two sets of silverware.

He quickly says, "Sorry, I made a mistake." He turns to leave, and she says, "No no, come in. Sit, sit." She guides him to an old armchair, the color of the red carpet in the hallway.

She sits on a sofa across from him and says, "We've lived here since 1972."

He wants to stand up. His eyes are drawn to the evidence of a worn-in home—pictures, an empty flower pot sitting by the window—things that were put in place and never moved again. A family that was together for a long time. He says, "I should go. I thought this was my apartment. But clearly it's not!"

She smiles at him, still peering serenely through her glasses. She looks over her shoulder and says, "He seems lost."

He smiles at her, confused by the person he hasn't seen yet. "Is your husband here?" He remembers an old couple at the tapas restaurant that night, eating fried potatoes in a tomato sauce with toothpicks. At the time, he imagined him and his wife getting old, having many unremarkable dinners together.

The woman yanks him back to the present. "My husband's been dead for 10 years. We still talk. The bond, you see, it's strong. He helps me through things." She rests her hands in her lap. "Do you talk to people who are gone?"

He feels pinpricks rolling across his arms. "What? Definitely not." He thinks about how he talks to his wife, late at night, apologizing, asking her to forgive him.

She says, "Maybe try it. It brings some peace. You know, the past isn't going anywhere."

Quickly, he pushes himself up out of the armchair, walks to the door, opens it, and says over his shoulder, "Well, thanks again, nice to meet you!" He hustles down the stairs and out onto the sidewalk, nearly tripping on the last step. He gets outside and doubles over, his hands on his knees, trying to catch his breath, feeling like he's going to vomit.

He needs to shake off the creepy old woman who talks to the dead. The next thing he knows, he's pressing the button for apartment 2 at the next building. A soft voice says, "Hello?"

"Hi, I think I used to live in this apartment, a while back, with my wife. Would you mind if I come up just to look around?"

"Hmm," the man says. "You're not a murderer or a cop or something, are you?"

Ray laughs. "I'm just a guy here for a conference." That seems to have done it, and he's buzzed in. Same carpet, same banister, same trip up the stairs.

The door to apartment 2 opens, and a tall, thin man stands there, in a white tank top and shorts, his blonde hair and pale skin making him look translucent.

He stares at Ray, who feels self-conscious in his gaze. All Ray can manage is, "Hi."

"So, you lived here?" The man flips his hair out of his eyes with the back of his hand.

"Yes," Ray says. "With my wife." He keeps mentioning his wife, to make him more relatable, but every time he mentions her, it's like a knife cutting him, a razor sharp memory that still draws blood.

The man sighs. "Okay, come in, I guess." It's a spartan apartment, with only a futon and a big drawing table covered with art supplies. The man, who looks about 25, sits on the futon, crosses his legs, then his arms, and looks at Ray, irritated.

Ray looks around. The kitchen is on the right side, not the left, like his apartment. As he turns to leave, the man says, "How long ago did you live here?"

Ray turns to the man with a puzzled look. "I think it was a different building on this street. Weird, right?"

"Not really," the man says. "All the buildings look the same. But it must not have been that great if you can't even remember the address."

"No, it was," Ray says, trying to will the past back with only the positive. "It was great!" His mind goes to him and his wife, strolling the Common, holding hands. He wants to cry. He pushes out the memories that butt in, the sight of his own blood dripping down his forehead as he sat upside down, the rotating police lights, the sirens.

The young man says, "This was the first place I found. I had to get away from my parents."

Ray laughs, attempting to bond with the young man. He says, "I know how that is."

The man doesn't move, his arms and legs remain crossed. "Did your parents ever tell you that you were 'rotten to the core'?"

Ray takes a step back. "Probably not exactly. But they thought I was an asshole."

"Yeah. Well, mine hate me." The man stands up and walks around Ray to the drawing table. "I moved into this place to get some space. To work on some stuff." Ray looks down at the drawings. They're all of menacing animals with sharp teeth, fierce looking, ready to attack. They're shaded in charcoal and pencil, smudged and monstrous.

The man says, staring at his drawings, "My folks are ashamed of me. So I just have to be invisible for a while."

"I'm sure they're not," Ray says, quickly. "I'm sure they love you." He thinks about how little he knows about love. "Just be yourself. And keep working on this stuff. Seriously. It's good."

"Thanks," the man says, without looking up. Ray backs toward the door slowly, imagining the wolf on the drawing coming to life, baring its teeth at him.

He moves out of the apartment wordlessly and walks slowly back down the stairs, massaging his temples. On the street, the sun is setting behind the buildings, the sky bluish purple. The shadows are growing longer on the sidewalk. He's disoriented, but feels a little jolt. He must keep going.

He's now at next building and when he presses the button for apartment 2, a raspy female voice briskly says, "What is it?"

Ray responds, "Hi. This sounds strange, but I used to live in your apartment, a while back, I think, with my wife. Probably before you lived here."

The woman snorts. "Oh yeah? How do you know how long I've lived here?"

He gives a forced laugh. "I'm in town for work. I'm trying to find my old apartment, to re-spark some memories. I think this is the building."

"You're not re-sparking anything here, buddy." After a moment, she continued. "I've lived here for 20 years. You sound lost. I get it, it's a crazy world. I don't really go out there. I'm here waiting for things to slow down a little bit."

Ray says, "Yeah, I get that. Everything happens really fast. Do you," he starts, then pauses. "Do you miss it out here? Out in the world?"

"It's a different kind of life," she says. "But it's a life. Anyway, see ya, buddy." With that, the intercom clicks off.

Ray's sober now. The day, and the trip, are weighing on him all at once. He can feel the knots in his shoulders. He thought that if he could see his old apartment, he could start to understand it all further. But now he's not sure. Maybe it's time to give up, he thinks.

The crash comes back, like it often does. He and his wife were driving back from dinner. He can see the two-lane road, brownish-green brush just off the edge, the sky deep orange as it goes behind the hills. He only takes his eye off the road for a second, to play a song for her. "Landslide," to make her smile. And just like that, a quick series of flips, cracks, and he's upside down. He doesn't remember looking over at her. He doesn't remember much beyond that. Just the song playing, *"and I'm getting older too,"* the sound of the ambulance, the aftermath.

Since then, he's been alone to deal with it all. For weeks, people were in and out of his house like ghosts, bringing food he never ate. Someone gave him an orchid, which seemed like a cruel joke, giving him the responsibility of keeping a plant alive. A friend suggested a therapist he could talk to. He didn't call. Now he's alone, in a city he doesn't live in, drunkenly knocking on people's doors. He had shaken off his hopelessness during this trip, but now it was back, in full force.

He stares at the brick building across the street, his elbows on his knees, chin resting on the palms of his hand. It's a windowless fortress of red that takes up the whole block. He's trying to remember what the building was used for, but his mind is blank.

He's nearly catatonic as he hears two people talking loudly. He turns and sees a man and a woman, both with thin builds and shoulder-length brown hair, walking toward him, sauntering like the photo from an album cover. The man is wearing shorts and a t-shirt, the woman a tie-died dress. He stares in astonishment, wondering how they look so much like each other.

They stop in front of the building next door, and see him staring.

The man says, "Do you live on Temple Street?"

Ray laughs. "Funny story. I thought I did."

They look at each other, communicating without saying a word. "Okay," the woman says, drawing the word out to five syllables. "Do you need help?"

His facade breaks down. "Honestly, I don't know. I was…looking for something."

"Huh," says the woman. "I'm Naomi. This is Sam." She points at the building. "Do you want to come up for some water? You don't look good."

He follows them up the same colored stairs, and, of course, to apartment 2. Naomi unlocks the door, and Ray follows them in. He watches their identical movements as they enter—the way they both take off their shoes by bringing their knees up to waist height, the way they take a deep breath and exhale loudly as they look around the apartment.

Naomi says, "Come in. Sit down." To the left is the kitchen, like his old apartment. He sits down in a wood chair at an old kitchen table. She hands him a glass of water, smiles, and leaves the small room. He takes a long drink and sets the glass down on the dark wood.

Through the opening in the kitchen wall, he can see the living room, and how discordant the apartment is with these two young people. Everything feels prehistoric. A vinyl sofa with brown cushions, heavy brown curtains on the windows, thick brown carpeting.

Sam and Naomi walk into the kitchen and sit down at the table, side by side, staring at him like it's an interrogation. Ray breaks the silence. "So, how long have you lived here?" He looks at them, back and forth, spreading his attention equally.

Naomi laughs. "Oh, this isn't our apartment. This is our dad's place. He passed away a few months ago. We're trying to figure out what to do with all this stuff."

Sam smiles. "We haven't done anything to it. It's how he liked it."

Naomi looks at Sam, then at Ray. "It's all pretty dreary, isn't it?"

Ray quickly says, "No. Seems nice. Authentic?"

Naomi gives him a sly look. "Authentic. Yeah." She looks at Ray. "So, what's your story?"

"I used to live on this street. I'm actually not sure where. I'm here for work. I've been going through some stuff. I thought seeing my old place would help. I've just been buzzing apartments, talking to people. Sounds insane, right? I have no idea what I'm doing, to tell you the truth."

The twins look at each other again. Sam says, "Sorry. That sounds kind of heavy."

Ray says, "It's been interesting. Met some characters."

"I bet," Naomi says. "Our dad would have had some stories for you. But we're just stuck here, watering that plant over there, like he's going to be back any day now."

Sam looks down, examining his long, delicate fingers. "I think he would have wanted us to keep the apartment." He looks at Naomi, who keeps her gaze fixed on Ray.

Naomi says, "So, are you going to keep knocking on doors until you find your old apartment?"

Ray shakes his head. "I'm really not sure. It's been intense, kind of fun, but now I feel kind of…sad again."

Naomi says, "Maybe it's this apartment. It's so sad. I could never come back, and that would be fine with me." Her mouth tightens, exactly as her brother's did before.

Sam looks at Ray, but is talking to Naomi. "We owe it to him. To keep this place. After everything that happened."

Naomi responds to Sam, also looking at Ray. "We don't owe him anything. He's not here anymore."

Ray has to play the mediator. "I'm sure he'd be fine with whatever you two decided. When my wife died, I wanted to throw everything out, immediately. That day, actually, I threw out a bunch of her shoes. Only shoes. There was still fresh laundry lying around. The house still *smelled* like her, the oil she used to put on in the morning. It was driving me nuts. But I went for the shoes. Piles and piles of them, I just stuffed them all into big, black garbage bags and threw them out the front door. It doesn't make sense now, but grief is strange like that."

Sam looks down, and says softly, "Sorry for your loss."

Ray looks back at Naomi. "Thank you. Could you maybe take the plant, and some of the other stuff, to one of your places? And sell this one?"

Sam pushes his chair back loudly and storms out of the kitchen. Naomi gives Ray a smile. "He thinks we have a responsibility to keep this place as a museum or something. We talk about it, but we can't make progress. We end up back here, just stumped."

Ray says, "It's tough, losing someone close."

Naomi doesn't look like she's listening. Maybe they forgot about his loss already. "We both missed phone calls from dad on the day he died. We were working. Sam can't get over it."

Ray says, "I understand. Guilt is a killer."

He wants to stay and spend more time with Naomi. He finds himself looking at her shoulders, where her t-shirt starts to fall to one side, and realizes he needs to get out of there.

He stands up quickly and says, "I'm so sorry about your dad. But I should go."

Naomi stands too, and says quietly, "Oh. Okay." She reaches up and touches his hand. "I'm sorry about your wife." He looks at her, and they hold each others's stare for a moment.

He pulls his hand back and walks out of the kitchen, and Sam's standing there. Ray could tell he had been listening to their conversation. He looks Sam in the eyes, and somehow feels comforted to see that he had the same eyes as she did, flecks of green and gold sparkling inside brown, shining in the hallway light. "She doesn't know how I feel," Sam says. "We both have to live with this."

Ray forces a smile and says, "I'm really sorry." He is sorry—for them, for himself. He feels claustrophobic and dizzy. He angles past Sam, opens the door, and bounds down the stairs. How many times has he run down stairs today?

Back on the street, it's dark, and the street lamps are shining isolated halos on the sidewalk. He has to get back to the hotel, to go back home. But to what? The prospect of going home, to the empty house, a huge hole in the middle of his life. Defeat sets in. This day has been a series of bizarre interactions, like Ray looking in a mirror, seeing himself the same as everyone he has met—broken and scattered.

He goes, almost unwittingly, up to the last building on the block, still thinking about Naomi and Sam, sitting silently, a vast sea of brown in between them. He pushes the buzzer for apartment 2.

A woman's voice answers. "Hello?"

Ray says, "Hi, I didn't mean to disturb you. I was in the neighborhood, I used to live on this block, and I'm wondering if I could just look into the apartment, just to see it?"

The woman replies, with a hesitant exhale, "I'm not sure that's a good idea."

"I understand," Ray says. "I get it. My wife, she and I used to live in the apartment, I think. I lost her recently. It just, it would mean a lot."

After a moment, the woman's voice says, again with a sigh, "Okay. Come up. For a minute."

He walks up the flight of stairs, and the door to apartment 2 is open. A small girl with pigtails stands in the door, squinting through glasses. "I'm Maggie," the girl says. "This is my mom, Laura." Behind her stands a woman, the mom, in a white sundress.

Ray leans down. "Hi Maggie, I'm Ray. Is it okay with you if I just look inside the apartment quickly?"

Maggie shrugs her shoulders and turns around. He follows her inside, and turns to Laura. "Thank you so much. Here's my business card. Just so you know that I'm a real person." Laura smiles at him, and Ray notices a dimple on the right side of her mouth. How strangely beautiful, he thinks.

As he walks inside, the apartment transforms in front of him, into the one that he used to live in. He takes a deep breath, trying to counter the lightheadedness. The memories hit him. Cooking in this kitchen. Stumbling in late at night. Carrying coffee to the bedroom, so many times. Dancing in the middle of the room to "Landslide," spinning on the old record player.

He stands there, while Maggie looks up at him. "So, you used to live here?"

Ray finally exhales. His voice catches. "Yeah, I did."

"Neat," Maggie says. She stands there, looking around like he does, seeing her current life, while he sees his former life. "Ray," Maggie says, "do you want to see something I'm working on?" Ray looks over at Laura, who nods.

He's trying to hold back the dam, barely keeping the force of his memories at bay. "Sure, yeah." Maggie sits down, cross-legged, next to a shoebox in the entryway. She pats the floor next to her, motioning for him to sit down. "It's a time capsule," Maggie says, looking up at him, smiling.

"Oh wow," Ray says. He sits down awkwardly, his back against the wall. "Very cool. What are you going to put in there?"

"Well," Maggie says, ready to explain. "My parents and I each put something really meaningful to us in here, and then in five years, we're going to open it back up, and see what we remember about the things that we put in there."

"That's excellent," Ray says, genuinely interested. "So, what did you put in there?"

"It's supposed to be something we have a strong memory about. So, my mom put in a Mother's Day card that I gave her, which she really loves. My dad put a cassette tape in there, from when he was younger. I think my mom gave it to him. Mom, is that right?" Laura nods again. "I'm putting this doll in there." She holds up a small doll, also a girl with pigtails.

"That is so cool," Ray says. "What do you think you'll see in here in five years?"

"I don't know," Maggie says. She looks at Laura again. "My mom says memories are important, but that sometimes we have to put them away to make room for new ones." She pauses, and looks at him. "You know, Ray, since you used to live in the apartment, and we're going to keep the time capsule here, maybe you can put something in, too?"

Ray gasps, and a half-laugh escapes. "Oh! I don't know if I should do that."

She says, in a serious voice, imitating an adult: "It's okay. If you give me something that's important to you, it's still yours. You don't have to forget it forever. But you can set it free."

Ray can now feel hot tears running down his cheeks. His hands are trembling. Without thinking, he reaches into his pocket and pulls out an earring.

A gold hoop. He carries it in his pocket everywhere he goes. "It was my wife's."

Maggie seems unfazed by a stranger sitting on her floor, crying. "Does she need it?"

Ray pauses and says, "No, not anymore."

Maggie looks at him with a neutral expression. "Well that's good. It seems like it's a memory you can put away. I'll take care of it. But now you've made room for a new one."

Ray scrambles to his feet, and manages to say, "Thank you. Bye, Maggie. Thank you, Laura." He rushes out of the apartment, down the stairs, and out of the building.

He stands in front of the building, looking down the block, seeing the street lamps, standing still, protective, like angels guarding the gates. He walks slowly to the end of Temple Street. He turns the corner without looking back.

Virgo Zodiac Highlight

Gentle Perfection

Rowan Quinn

Every detail holds significance, no matter how
small
a keen eye noticing what others overlook,
an innate desire to improve, to refine, to perfect.

Patience is woven into the fabric of daily life,
a steady rhythm that guides gentle corrections,
a quiet commitment to order, to service.

There is an ease in structure, a comfort in routine,
yet beneath it all, a restless pursuit of betterment,
an understanding that growth is in the careful steps
taken.

Compassion manifests in acts of usefulness,
a silent dedication to making things right,
a humility that values effort over praise.

In the stillness, there is strength, resilient and
unwavering
a quiet force that shapes the world with meticulous
care.

Aunt Lalena

Douglas Young

Miles had never felt close to his Aunt Lalena, but it struck him driving to her house that every interaction he had ever had with her was positive. Though he had generally only seen her at big family get-togethers, it now occurred to him that she had always been unfailingly kind, pleasant, an avid listener, supportive of whatever he said, and never intrusive. He was particularly grateful for all the times she quietly sought him out at family events when he was at his most adolescently awkward to ask how he was doing, encourage him, and make him feel like he had at least one confirmed fan among his extended family clan.

Unlike all his other aunts and uncles who married and had children, Aunt Lalena was the family's old maid who lived alone. He winced at how seldom he and his family had visited her, preferring instead the company of kin whose houses were full of cousins. In conversations with relatives over the years, Aunt Lalena was the most often missing and least often mentioned.

Now she was quite old and dying. Though Miles had dreaded the two-hour drive to say goodbye, he knew he would feel guilty if he failed to go. Even though he understood she was now usually asleep, he could still visit with the relatives who were looking after her. He could also listen to music en route and reminisce about a relation who he had never really thought much about.

It seemed to him that Aunt Lalena bore a heavy load of shyness. She got on well with everyone but appeared close to none. In a large family tree full of loud and lively branches, hers was decidedly still and quiet. Though she would immediately smile and reply when spoken to, she remained a mostly silent figure in the background, always an extra or, at best, a bit or supporting player. No one had an unkind word to say about such an eternally gracious lady, but Aunt Lalena's life defined inconspicuous: an assistant at her local public library, a dutiful attendee at church, and a modest presence at family gatherings.

She lived alone with her cat in an immaculately well kept, small home. Miles recalled when, growing up, his family had stopped by her house for a quick, unannounced visit on the way back from somewhere and Aunt Lalena saw him admiring her rolltop desk. She apologized for how "messy" the antique was despite it being far more orderly than his family's rolltop and her not knowing they would visit that day. But, as Aunt Lalena liked to say, "It's always good to see you."

Though she had a ready smile, he tried to recall ever seeing her laugh boisterously or lose herself in animated conversation. On the plus side, of all his many aunts and uncles, only Aunt Lalena had never inflicted unwanted advice upon her nephews and nieces, but he and his cousins still saw her as too proper to confide in when they did not want to talk with their parents about something. *Maybe we just didn't give her a chance,* he wondered. *Perhaps she would have welcomed being included in some family secrets. That might have spiced up her overly dull plotline. Was hers a train wreck of a tragically lonely life, and did I contribute to that loneliness by not visiting her more?* He sighed nearing her home.

And now it's all too late, he reflected. *At least everyone loved her*, he tried to comfort himself while feeling weird to think of her in the past tense. He hoped she knew how loved she was and, though she had lived her entire adult life by herself, Miles was grateful that a few relations were staying with her around the clock, along with hospice nurses, so that she could remain home and not die alone. And she was very old, he consoled himself. *Who wants to reach the stage when having a bowel movement counts as an achievement?* he rationalized.

Pulling into Aunt Lalena's driveway, he marveled at her spotless and still shiny twenty-five-year-old car. But he got a little nervous at the sight of a pair of other cars. In a contemplative mood, he wanted to spend time alone with his dying aunt and dreaded sharing their final moments together with others, especially since there was a lot he wanted to say in confidence.

At the front porch door, he was greeted by one of Aunt Lalena's sisters, his Aunt Amoreena, and her daughter Zelia, nicknamed Zelie, a favorite cousin.

"Well, nephew, dog if you ain't absolutely ageless," Aunt Amoreena exclaimed after a big hug and kiss. "You Oscar Wilde's Dorian Gray, are you? Boy, you don't even look thirty."

"With all due respect, Aunt Amoreena," he replied, "I believe you may need to see your eye doctor. When I turn around, y'all can see my rapidly expanding bald spot too. Actually, I'm 39 plus considerable interest."

"Well, Cuz, you sure hide it well," Cousin Zelia remarked while embracing him.

"How's Aunt Lalena?" he asked gently.

"Well," Aunt Amoreena sighed, "she's holding steady. She's always had such a quiet strength. She hasn't spoken in a couple of days and just sleeps, but she seems comfortable."

"I sure hope she's not in any pain," he stated as a question.

"Oh, good Lord, no, child." Aunt Amoreena chuckled. "She's so doped up on morphine that the nurses say there ain't no way she's hurting any. Come on back to the bedroom and sit with her a spell. We just bathed and changed her."

"Oh, gosh. Is she decent? I don't want to intrude," he noted.

"Oh, sure, shug." His aunt laughed.

The bedroom was dark except for a little lamp turned on by the bed to reveal Aunt Lalena asleep with a cross around her neck and her mouth slightly ajar. Her arms lay by her side above the covers, and her nightgown looked a couple of sizes too big.

"Have a seat, darling," Aunt Amoreena said motioning to the bedside chair. "Zelie and I'll be just down the hall if you need anything."

Seated alone with his least obtrusive relative, he looked at Aunt Lalena, not sure what to say or do. He was taken aback by the hollowness of her cheeks and how bony her hands had become. He was further struck by several moles on her forehead not noticed before.

"Aunt Lalena," he mustered in a voice slightly above a whisper as he leaned toward her, "it's your nephew Miles." He paused. "I hope you can hear or understand me."

There was no movement on the bed or any change in her expression. He looked at the walls to see traditional paintings of rural landscapes, embroidered Biblical scriptures and crosses, and framed pictures of various kin. Not knowing what to say, he slowly reached over to hold her left hand. When her fingers wrapped around his, he started slightly.

"Can you hear me, Aunt Lalena?" he asked excitedly, but there was no reply. He thought of all the things he had ever wondered about her, like whether she had ever dated, done anything wild, or what she really thought of certain obnoxious relatives behind that placid smile. He also recalled the last time he was left alone with her as a boy one afternoon and feeling nervous making small talk amidst the quiet.

He was startled when his aunt's black cat jumped on the bed, looked at him, nestled against his aunt's side, and soon began to purr. Miles returned his gaze to his aunt's face. Reminding himself that he would never get another chance to talk with her, and reassured that no one else could hear, he finally spoke.

"Aunt Lalena, I'm real sorry you've had such a terribly tough time of late, and I'm right sorry I haven't visited you sooner. I hope Aunt Amoreena told you I called, and hopefully she read my letter to you. Actually, truth be told, Aunt Lalena, I'm sorry I didn't – haven't – visited you more all along. You've always been the most consistently kind—"

He stopped to avoid crying, looking at her closed eyes and motionless, emaciated body. Moving his tongue around his mouth, he then spoke again.

"Aunt Lalena, now that I think back, you may be the sweetest relative I've ever known, always with a friendly word and never moody, bringing your ever-delicious sweet potato pie to family reunions, sending a card every birthday, coming to all my graduations, and even driving all the way over to visit me when I was in the hospital—”

He quickly turned away and blinked several times before swallowing and taking a deep breath.

“You’ve just always been there for everyone, Aunt Lalena,” he whispered before clearing his throat. “Whenever we all got together or anyone needed anything, you were there.” He paused and noticed one wall was full of pictures of their relatives, including his family’s church portrait and graduation pictures of himself and all his siblings and cousins. He looked back at her and swallowed.

“Thank you, Aunt Lalena. Thank you ever so much for all you’ve done for each of us – for all your love…. And we all love you, Aunt Lalena. I love you too….”

He squeezed her hand gently and felt no response. He felt the urge to blow his nose but refrained.

Not knowing what else to say, and knowing how faithful his aunt was, he decided to pray, recalling the time when he was little that she had recited his bedtime prayers with him.

Now holding her hand in both of his with his head bowed, he spoke softly.

“Dear Heavenly Father, we come to you on behalf of one of the finest servants of yours I’ve ever known. Thank you very much for all your blessings for dear Aunt Lalena. Indeed, you’ve given her a mighty long and super respectful life, a life rich in service to others, a life defined by selflessness. In fact, she’s always been such an example for us all. Dear Lord, she really needs you now, and we beseech thee to please grant her peace and tranquility as she prepares to meet you. Thank you for the wonderfully inspiring life of love and service that she has given us all, and please ease her transition into your kingdom. In Christ's name we pray. Amen."

Miles slowly raised his head and looked at the blank face before him. He noted her steady breathing and then heard the cat purring. Looking at the cat, he caught himself smile and quickly stifled it, blinking and turning back to his aunt.

"I wish I could hold hands with your thoughts, Aunt Lalena."

Unable to think of anything else to say, he surveyed the room one last time before gazing at his aunt's face. Though filled with sadness at what he feared may have been an unfulfilled life lived alone, as well as much regret for not having been a bigger part of it, he felt a sense of calm entirely absent when he arrived. He slowly leaned forward to kiss her forehead.

"Love you, Aunt Lalena," he said as he released her hand and stood. Looking back seemed anticlimactic, so he did not. Instead, he slowly left the room, gently closing the door behind him.

He could not remember the subsequent small talk with Aunt Amoreena and Cousin Zelia, but knew it was all cheerful and that they thanked him for coming. It was comforting to learn that many other relatives had visited as well, and he hoped Aunt Lalena knew it.

On the drive home, he did not play music for a long time. Instead, he tried hard to rewind and play back all his memories of Aunt Lalena from earliest childhood forward. He wanted to believe she really had been happy behind all the sweet smiles at family gatherings. He wished he had known her better and that she had made a family of her own. *But who am I to say she wasn't content as she was?* he asked. *With all the stressful drama in so many of our relations' lives, including mine, who's to say hers wasn't a model of serene stability? It's all past tense now anyway. Surely if there's a just God, she's Heaven-bound. If Aunt Lalena doesn't qualify, who does? So, however happy or unhappy she was, she'll soon be in Heaven or at least completely free of all pain and loneliness.*

He stared in the distance a long time before making a resolution.

Never refrain from telling someone I love her and appreciate her, and go visit her because ... "*it's always good to see you.*"

Black and White: *In Memory of Hayden Potter*

John RC Potter

My favourite photo of you,
now and before you left us,
is the one of you standing
in a doorway, leaning casually;
A black and white photo
of a handsome young man
with his life ahead of him.
But that was taken from you
before your time.
Or what it your time?
For the rest of my life,
you will forever be standing
in that distant doorway:
Waiting for something, or someone.

First you lost your mother, far too young.
Then you were given up for dead
after a horrible car accident;
But you climbed and clawed
your way back into the world,
toward the flickering light.
Your life was never the same,
but you never complained.
A survivor, and yet, for too few years.
Those years flashed by in a blink of an eye.
Only a quarter of a century
you were given, then
you were taken in your sleep,
like your mother before you.

Our world is not black and white.

The years ahead will be long and wide,
whilst you are close by on the other side
of the vast unknown and the great divide.

September Full Moon Special

Harold Versus the Librarians

Donna Lormand

Harold refused to move. The air vent in front of the Self-Help section was his at night, and everyone knew it.

"Fine, Harold." Regina pinched the bridge of her nose. "I'll get the book in the morning." Harold had thwarted her once again.

"Told you she wouldn't make it," I murmured to Val, who forked over a one-dollar bill. She'd made the last-minute online request under her granddaughter's profile so Regina wouldn't know, and we'd taken bets on whether Regina would be fast enough.

"Closing time," Regina called, shooing the group of us milling around gently out of the main hall through the double doors and out into the courtyard. "Have a good night," she called over her shoulder to Harold before turning off all the lights and locking up.

"See you all tomorrow," Regina waved as she headed down the sidewalk.

"She almost had him," Chuck said, waving his a one-dollar bill in my face. I plucked it from his fingers.

"Sit down, you old fossil," I grumbled and pointed to the stone table we sat around most nights after Regina kicked us out.

This table had heard much speculation about Harold. Why, for example, had he chosen the Self-Help section? Why not, we questioned, Science Fiction or Mysteries, since these seemed better suited to his situation? Trying to figure out how he would have self-classified if the library still used the Dewey Decimal System had taken up an entire week and we fared no better, even with all those extra categories.

In all likelihood, the choice was probably practical. It was a prime spot that was warm in winter and cool in summer, and if one was quiet, as one should be in a library, one could sometimes catch snippets of whispered conversations. Not that Harold, or anyone, spied. I'm just noting the acoustics.

Harold was a collector of things.
Old things and new things.
Plush things. Brittle things.
Sticky things and things that smelled.
Unloved things.
…
Sometimes much-loved things.
…
We seniors respect this. A good collection is a work of art.

Harold had been there since before any of us, even Regina, who was here when we were children. She should be retired with us, playing bingo every Tuesday in the library upstairs instead of running it, but it made her happy and who are we to get in her way?

Harold was so called because of the weathered and fading "Hi, my name is _Harold_" sticker plastered to his front, which every now and then someone traced over with permanent marker to ensure it could still be read. No one ever tried to change the name. The use of "he" was also haphazard. When asked if that was his preferred pronoun, Harold declined to respond, as he did for all options, which greatly distressed the youths.

Moreover, no one could puzzle out how he'd gotten in. Rumor has it that he was just there one cold winter morning, causing quite a fright for the head librarian at the time. Some said that a fired librarian had wheeled Harold there out of spite, but that didn't seem plausible, for many reasons, none less than that librarians aren't known for their physical prowess, that Harold was incredibly heavy, and that librarians are never fired. Some said Harold was requested via interlibrary loan, but there was no record of such a loan request, and librarians are excellent record keepers. Others postulated that it was a prank orchestrated by the youths, but none of them claimed it and those entitled little turds certainly would have. The only person who might have been able to explain was old man Wilson, but he died last spring; and honestly, his memory had gone in the end and no one could decide which of his tales were real and which were of a mind gone feral and unraveled anyway.

It didn't really matter.

Harold was here, and though they'd tried every possible way, the librarians could not get him out. Wheeling him straight out the double front doors hadn't worked; he was an inch too big. They'd removed the doors from the hinges, which should have given them enough space, but when they tried again, Harold was suddenly an extra inch bigger.

"Did you measure thrice and check twice?" Chuck had asked, to which a very annoyed Regina had replied "Yes, Chuck," through her gritted teeth.

They'd tried turning him on his side various ways, even diagonal, but he'd stick to the floor like he'd been glued there with construction grade glue, shuddering and belching noxious fumes, until they promised to right him. A removal company, the librarians' last hope, had also failed—all their tools for cutting and sawing mysteriously ceasing to work when they came within a hundred feet of the library. In the end, Tom, the company owner, had to apologize for his inability to help and had refunded the library's money. The librarians threw up their hands and shrugged. Harold was there to stay. But, although he gave the librarians something to complain about—and we all know librarians love to complain—they made sure to tell him "good morning" and "good night" every day and they fretted about him on federal holidays when the library was closed. We know they fretted because I once overheard Regina telling another librarian about how much she'd worried. I wasn't spying. The acoustics carry, which I've already noted.

When Harold wasn't near the air vent, he was usually in the lobby, snuggled next to Regina's desk. She mostly ignored him, but when she needed to get in or out of her desk, she'd have to squish herself to the wall to get around his inconveniently wide perimeter.

"Harold!" she'd slam her hands to her hips in momentary exasperation then sigh and smile slightly. It was the smile she used when she talked about Tom. They were dating thanks to the Harold Debacle, and she'd sigh and pat Harold's side as she squeezed past.

On Saturday mornings, Harold could be found occupying a corner of the children's room on the second floor. Occupied is definitely the right word, given that Harold was way too large and boxy for the corner and given that no one had any idea how he got there, what with his wheels and the stairs and that he was a "trash receptacle" (name calling is rude) way too large for the elevator.

The children, however, found him fascinating. They'd stare with their big round eyes and complete lack of manners. On one especially inspired craft day, the children had covered Harold in googly eyes, so now it seemed like he was watching you from all angles, a real Dali meets Mona Lisa kind of vibe (a word the youths recently taught us!). And though Harold sometimes smelled, the children looked forward to sharing story time with him, making sure he got to see any pictures in the books and squealing with delight when Harold gave a little shudder of gratitude, his collection rattling inside. Sometimes Harold even shared something he had collected with them, opening the sliding door on his side and shooting out a treasure like an air cannon–fired t-shirt at a sporting event. The stuffed animals were a favorite.

The only other place Harold frequented was the roof, but only on very clear nights, when the stars were bright and the moon full and the city haze lifted enough for the sky to be considered clear. Although this was rare, tonight was such a night, and indeed we could just make out Harold's wheels dangling over the edge like the feet of some giddy and foolish teenager.

"What do you think he's doing up there?" Val asked, as someone from our group always did when this happened. Theories abounded, but hostile library takeover and anti-capitalist sit-in were the favorites. Some swore they could hear the librarians up there with him, baying wildly at the moon, which would indicate that it was actually Harold AND the librarians not Harold VERSUS the librarians. But this was clearly impossible. Even if they were in cahoots, librarians go to bed at 8pm sharp and it was always well past 8.

Me, personally?

I think that Harold

just every now and then

wants to feel the exhilaration of being a little too close to the edge of something

and the interconnected insignificance of being under all those stars.

The End.

Half-Eaten Falafel on a Bus Stop Bench

Michael Roque

**Do you ever feel like a half-eaten falafel
abandoned on a bus stop bench at 3AM?**

Traffic dies down,
people stop passing by,
you're sat half-consumed—
a stale pita lost to the anticipation of a next bite,
wondering why you weren't finished.

Did the purchaser think you weren't good enough?
That you lacked taste?
Maybe you made them feel too full—
too much for them to stomach?
Too spicy for their senses,
perhaps they didn't want the fragrance of your
amba
sticking to their fingers?

**Maybe sometimes you're more bike than man—
fastened to a Florentin pole.**

Locked for months,
wheels and seat stolen—
you're little more than a rusted steel frame
wondering if you'll ever ride again,

experience the wind you can barely recall
that blew through your gears.

**Maybe you're an umbrella
slammed out of shape by pounding showers.**

Left bent and dilapidated
in a puddle,
recognizing in water's reflection
a defective product,
who couldn't weather the rain—
shelter from the storm.
Snapped plastic wondering why—
why you were dumped into the gutter,
deemed unworthy of repair?

The Mystery of the Wife of Bath

Kavitha Reddy Goyal

Thea picked up her pace muttering 'damn' under her breath, hers was the last classroom. She hurriedly rounded the left turn into the glass bookcase-lined double-wide hallway of the English Department just in time to see Susie's brown curls disappear around the edge of the heavy mahogany door as it swung shut.

Sr. Mary Gertrude, the Directress of Upper School, stepped into Thea's path about fifteen feet in front heading the same direction, arms laden with piano books. Thea inhaled sharply, pausing her stomping assault on the ancient oak floorboards. She was in for it now, she thought, late for World Literature, and moving like an all-terrain vehicle across the Mojave, rather than a finishing school ninth grader.

What a piece of sanctimonious work, Sr. Mary Gertrude Fordham, but oh– were those calves fine. Ruffle-collared striped shirt cinched perfectly into butt-hugging Italian wool pencil skirt in slate gray, and the clincher– four-inch peep toe stilettos, in matching gray leather. In 1983, nuns in the Bleeding Order of the Holy Blah Blah Blah no longer had to wear all black, but were they actually allowed to be sexy? The faint silky hose, warm sheen, covered the shapely muscles and so-slim ankles. Only one way to get *that* kind of buff. How did a nun get to go to the gym - a mystery - the free time between mindful prayer sessions.

Tell-tale creaking announced Thea's tardiness. Sister Mary Gertrude effortlessly swirled hundred-eighty on one icepick pump and delicately hovered the other one with toes flirting upward.

Heart nearly pounding out of her ribcage, Thea froze. If called a third time into the Directress's office in one semester, she would surely lose her scholarship and have to switch to Lincoln Public mid-school year.

She had been skating precariously with her folks, twice chastened this semester already. Last time, grounded for a month after she had stolen pages of perforated hot lunch tickets from Sr. Bernadette's top drawer when she fell asleep at her desk in the middle of European History. It was simply irresistible, the way her huge round head lolled onto the pillow created by her crossed hands resting in turn on a billowy drooping chest, so that only the bottom inch of the heavy silver cross on her blouse front was visible below the slack mouth under a haired lip. Becca sketched the priceless strip of comedy live from a central vantage point within the classroom. The other girls had silently egged Thea on, eyebrows ferociously mouthing 'do it!'

"You're late again, Thea," unmoving lines for lips released the statement, stern-jawed, while steely blue orbs punctured her veneer. It was remarkable how Sr. Mary Gertrude's face, so devoid of color and charm, managed to convey cold, powerful beauty.

Thea was in good company, even the upper-class girls quaked in their penny loafers should MGF cast a chilling lizard eye in their direction. Perky blonde bob, athletic form, you could believe she was any age from twenty-nine to fifty-nine. No one knew how she went from piano teacher to Head Mistress of a prominent school in a day, or how she never faltered, saying exactly the right thing to parents, community members, diocese leaders, and other nuns. And she looked badass while doing it, with unapologetic posture and not a minute to spare from important decisions of running the hundred and sixty-year-old girls' preparatory school in a gorgeous, sprawling Georgian red brick that caused board members of Connecticut's historic register to drool.

"I'm sorry, Sister," Thea stammered in pink tones, as she rushed past "Iron Heels," the statuesque disciplinista, floating a whiff of floral petals, and slammed herself with her own backpack while trying to slip it off and open the classroom door at the same time.

The hefty door closed more loudly than intended, an unfortunate feature of the prior century's construction, either gentle latch click to ensure it wouldn't slide back open or big bang, nothing in between. The girls jumped in their seats while attempting to hide giggles. Up front Miss Myrtle Winthrop's chin went lax.

"Kindly take a seat," an eyebrow shot up over the scarlet readers.

In the seat saved for her, Thea pulled out her English notebook and pencil, not daring to link eyes with Susie, Jane, Savitri or Becca who formed the immediate chair-wide perimeter, for risk of erupting in uncontrollable snickers. She pushed her auburn bangs out of her eyes, evened her breathing and instead trained her eyes at the front of the classroom. Ms. Winthrop's ample middle-aged form, clad in homely brown cardigan and long chaste skirt, that could have stood erect even starchless, was wrestling with a dwindling piece of chalk to highlight the key themes of "The Wife of Bath's Tale."

Miss Winthrop waddled around to face the room, with Chaucer's *The Canterbury Tales* cocked open in her left hand, and chalk clutched in a powdery right hand. Her bowl-cut pewter hair was deeply side-parted and pinned with a plastic barrette. How did she not know that barrettes were for females under the age of five? As she spoke ardently, spittle collected in the corners of her forever down-turned mouth. She must have felt it, wiping with her hand, depositing more chalk dust on a furry white cheek.

Thea let a glance slip at Becca on her left, and they each used every one of the forty-three facial muscles to suppress laughter over the cartoon sketch in progress. A gentle nudge from Savitri on the outside of her right forearm served to focus Thea's self-control as she surreptitiously passed her left hand under the crook of her right elbow to accept the tiny folded note. Then began the covert procedure of uncurling and decoding the microscopic missive, not unlike tweezer defusing a bomb on their beloved show '*Mission Impossible*.' It read 'MW=WM-M+W(MGF).'

She sent Sav a look of exaggerated confusion, wondering how this riddle tied in with the girls' typical ribbing of Myrtle Winthrop, ungenerously pegged as a loveless hippie matron, whose unabashed passion for literature seemed without fail to uncover if not invent sexual innuendo in whatever text was under discussion.

Myrtle's throaty voice hiccupped with excitement, "Many would call her progressive, a women's libber, centuries before her time! She's got opinions on a woman's role in marriage, about sex, power play, role in the Church—" her tone dropped an octave and decelerated, "What, pray tell, is so funny, Thea?"

Thea's stomach jumped into her mouth— had she seen the note? Unblinking, she slid her left hand clenched sweaty with the paper scrap down to the negligible space between the wooden seat and her rear end. "No, not funny, Ms. Winthrop. I was just thinking about the Knight and why he—"

"Why don't you bring whatever's in your left hand up front, you can lay it right on top of the piano." Her usually good-natured chubby face became an implacable mask.

Thea paled several shades. Imploring Savitri with a piteous permission-seeking glance, she trudged the gauntlet to the front of the classroom All eyes on her, ears rang white-hot as if they would explode. Chalk dust produced a sneeze fit for an ogre and startled her back to thinking mode. She would be ousted, her parents would not let her see the light of day after this.

She woodenly turned to face her classmates, gravitas before the executioner's swing, unworthy- yet awaiting- a Hail Mary. When none came, she placed the unintelligible shred of evidence on the glossy black hood of the baby grand and returned to her seat, slumped in fear of the wrath of Sr. Mary Gertrude, logarithmically worse than what her parents would serve up.

"Tomorrow, we'll discuss our gap-toothed heroine's commentary on sexual freedom, and any potential references to non-traditional love."

Eyes around the room rolled.

Thea thought to herself, now that was a mystery- the Wife of Bath liked women too?

At the end of class, Ms. Winthrop motioned Thea to remain.

Sixteen classmates filed out slower than a dirge, sending prayers of a sort: Susie, Jane, Becca, and Savitri last, her beautiful tawny face scrunched in sadness and shaded with guilt.

"Who passed you the note?" Ms. Winthrop stood close enough to waft warm breath laced with cigarettes and stale coffee onto her student.

"I don't know, I just felt a nudge." She fidgeted, laying flat the pleats of the short plaid polyester uniform skirt.

"Thea, what does the note mean?" She pulled off the glasses and stared her down, lines of her face furrowed deep.

"I have no idea, Ms. Winthrop," she edged backwards.

"So that's how we'll play this game, is it?"

#

The meeting was set for Thursday, two days after the incident, at 3:30 pm in the Head Mistress' office with her parents, and the Guidance Counselor, Sister Mary Constance. Apparently, Ms. Winthrop had already fully communicated her input. No other students had to be there because Thea had not offered up any implicating information. She didn't know if the note was going to make an appearance.

Lunch on Wednesday at their usual large rough-hewn wooden dining table in the far back left of the cafeteria was a somber affair. Thea idly stabbed her fork at beef tomato macaroni casserole, normally a favorite, while soggy green beans remained untouched.

Becca took a bite of her cheeseburger, "You don't think she'll pull the scholarship?"

Thea stared heavy-lidded.

Jane said, "Nah. You play violin with the local symphony and your grades are awesome. She'll come up with something more creative to make you suffer."

"Jesus, Jane," said Becca, eyebrows joining as one.

Jane shrugged innocently.

"Constance will stick up for you."

"Fat chance, no way she'll cross Iron Heels."

"What's the big fucking deal, just a note," said Sav.

All eyes turned to her not saying what they were thinking.

Susie arrived with a lunch tray bearing no lunch, but five little plates of plastic wrapped freshly baked soft in the center double chocolate-chip cookies that had just been birthed into the dessert station. These were cookies of legend, baked daily for the students' lunch. By heaven-sent buttery aroma *alone* they nearly balanced the scales against the repressive atmosphere of the Blessed Convent of Parma. Then there was the incomparable, euphoric taste of these delectables, which for the moment made the girls forget the rigid creativity-squashing moral and behavioral code of their school environment. Three minutes later not a crumb remained.

"Exactly, remember when Susie snuck out during Liturgy and went up the secret stairs to the Dome above the Cathedral?"

Chuckles. "Or when Jane walked onto the flat tiled roof outside Latin class because Rabbi Myers never showed up for class?"

Giggles, "What about when Thea pretended to pass out in World Religions to get out of the quiz?" A few more escapades were re-lived, putatively more mischievous than the matter at hand.

"This ain't no big."

Thea was not reassured, "Guys, what if I have to go to Lincoln?"

Silence blanketed the friends.

#

Later that afternoon, Thea was subdued by nerves but grateful when Jane offered to meet her during Library period to do homework. They chewed gum aggressively and exchanged looks of panic alternating with support while writing out their study notes. Thea also chewed on a strand of long russet hair, and woefully got the gum stuck in it. In the fifteen-minute break between Library and European History, they hit the restroom and then went for an inside walk, as freshmen were not allowed on the Smoking Porch and it was too damp for the school's grounds. Taciturn, they sauntered down the dim back hallways.

Their path took them by Sr. Mary Gertrude's spacious office, familiar for its soft lighting from the green shaded desk lamp and misleadingly inviting leather couches. The door was strangely ajar, someone hadn't clicked it closed. Thea first saw the black pumps, casually tossed to the side on the exquisite Persian carpet. Her breath caught. Eyes nearly popped out of her head as they next landed on an image burned into the retinas for her remaining days on earth. Iron Heels and Myrtle were locked in an embrace and passionate kiss, leaning against the front of the desk.

Jane in turn, noting the shift in Thea's body language, immobilized silently into an awkward twist to afford a view into the little tableau as she passed the door slit.

"Holy Shit!" they mouthed to each other, the whites of their eyes visible all-round.

Thea, emboldened by a nascent creativity bubbling deep within her young soul, let the oak planks creak ever so slightly as she turned to pass yet again by the cracked door, overtly making her presence known while peering inward. She willed her eyebrows stay put, and her expression remain placid. The effect was immediate, and the objective easily accomplished- her two educators sprang apart in anguish, one white as paper, the other a robust crimson.

It was a mystery- what went on behind doors thought to be closed.

The girls turned back around. With casual pace and audible footfall, they made their way down stately wood-paneled hallways to European History, hearts pounding out of their chests, laughter powerfully suppressed as a pin holds a grenade.

#

Thursday's meeting arrived with nary a second thought, let alone trepidation. Thea met her parents at the Visitor's entry at 3:25. The volunteer student at the desk had the radio on low playing the latest top forty, Michael Jackson's *"Beat It."*

"Why did she need to see us today?" her father asked.

"Just routine. I think they like to check in sometimes with all the students getting scholarships." Thea was nonplussed, even sheepish, a contrast from the dread pall of two nights ago, as she showed them a few historic features of the elegant Front Hallway.

"Hmff," said her father.

"Well, that's just lovely," said her mother.

Sister Mary Constance, of short and heavy stature, in a long black skirt, met them at 3:28 to usher them into the period Drawing Room, furnished with graceful velvet settees and sumptuous cascading drapes in ochre and muted azure, and scented with lavender potpourri. Gilt frames adorned three walls not bearing windows, balding white men of the cloth, be it black or red, and a couple of pastoral oils.

Sr. Mary Gertrude arrived at 3:31, also muted in attire, white lawn shirt buttoned up to the chin, silver cross on heavy chain hung half-way down her chest, and an A-line charcoal skirt with non-descript flats. Perhaps a touch discomfited, wondered Thea, having noticed both the extra minute, unprecedented in the fastidious Directress, and an unusual downward slant of her facial features.

Brief opening remarks commenced, and extra niceties were piped in by Sister Mary Constance.

Thea trained her eyes on the Head Mistress unflinchingly. What was she saying? Something about appreciation of Thea's academic and musical accomplishments. Thea sat bare knees crossed under hands daintily clasped, as she cocked her head at her parents with a closed lip smile and occasional eye lash flutter. Her mind raced over opportunities for demands for fun and freedoms at home. Like the Wife of Bath said, women should get their own way.

Head Mistress was saying that she saw no impediment to renewal of the scholarship throughout the remaining high school years- they could also consider waiving the work study portion, provided, of course, that Thea maintained her academic standing, just a perfunctory requirement, of course, given her exemplary performance to date, of course. At 3:35, she wrapped the session with noting how pleased she was, of course, that the family had come in to hear the good news in person.

September New Moon Special

Time

T. B. Vittini

after R. S. Thomas

The physicist in Marseille says: it is an illusion;
another in Ontario: it is fundamental and
irreversible;
the philosopher in Stockholm: every moment
disappearing;
in Oslo: every moment precious.

So,
what is this puzzle, time?

Now, we say,
as it already ceases to be,
looking at luminous stars
that are black holes,
beneath a night sky that is morning
in the Azores.

I could see bruises

beneath raging blisters on
her feet, the blue toes
curled into themselves like heads
of dead flowers.

I watched her splutter and drool
attempting to answer
our uneasy chatter, writhing
day and night beneath the sheets,
persistent in her plaintive bleating.

What point is there
in wrestling with this matter,
time,
deducing this or that,
no nearer to the very heart,
when it can't undo
her agonizing twilight?

Baldur's Saga

A J Dalton

The welcome of his hall was famous
for many a wand'ring thane
found honor at his table
and mead at his fireside
then a place-share on his long-boat—
Hringhorn, the greatest treasure-ship ever known—
So fair and wise was the shining prince Baldur
all knew Asgard would be tragic without him
thus mother-Frigg made all things vow never to do
him harm
and so it was, so readily was it bound.

Then our bright son sought to amuse his blind
brother Hoth, and others
having them deadly hurl weapons to no avail
all objects turning away from any killing blow
and much was the beholding wonder and joy
till the jealous Loki came stealing in
to plant a strange spear in his unseeing kin's hand
a lance of mistletoe too newly born for adult
promise—
all innocent did it pierce our hero's great heart—
through tears brave Vali grief-slew the unsighted
warrior
bringing overwhelming darkness to host,
Breidablik-home and lands far and wide.

Then Odin King knelt to raise his fondest child up
ferrying him to fiery Hringhorn as floating pyre
whispering the unknowable at his ear
bestowing the magical ring of return, Draupnir

still unable to deny wife-Nanna and horse joining
the noble loss
—yet the flames would not devour any
till Thor's Mjolnir forced that furnace
—and Hel swore not to allow passage to her realm
if all wept for the slain: alas,
the stubborn giantess Thokk, now Loki-touched,
could not!

Thus the glory of what had been was no more
so the days were dark and long
as were the people silent and hang-headed
knowing that they were in fell times
that would only see Ragnarök come:
All will be undone, though all will be set free–
Baldur will find the way from Niflheim
Hoth will be thrown out of death's castle-prison
Vali will leave Valhalla's feast
And they will be reconciled, their rule made anew.

The Lament of Hector

A J Dalton

Why must I slaughter
So many Greeks–
Because my brother loved too well,
Because Venus is cruel,
Because our foe knows no proportion?

Achilles burns to face me
With an ill-matched desire, they say
His ardor is too great, so
Let him abide with his spear-carrier
Patroclus, for a while.

Ah no, I slew his bannerman
And so he swears he'll be revenged
Driven by the very sort of passion
That saw this war begin
When Paris freed Helen from her spouse.

It seems our giddy tryst
Will end families, cities and states
Such a small thing to cause
All this – the gods must think us
Justly tragic entertainment.

Full thirty heroes I've killed
Their armor and slaves now mine
I wish such honor would recompense
The enemy, so that Troy might live
Yet for that I fear I must die.

Jupiter

A J Dalton

Honor me, mortal
For it is my due
Court not my displeasure
Or my wrath will befall you
Your house will be toppled
Your children undone
Your crops will be withered
And your herds will then sicken.

Rightly fear me, mortal
And learn to know your place
Dare not challenge the gods
Or you'll damn your whole race
Your towns will be buried
By volcano, sea and quake
Your islands will drown
Your history erased.

Come celebrate me, mortal
In music, dance and ode
Build my statues and temples
My transport and roads
So armies can march
To spread the good word
My empire is come
And my will must be done.

Assassination

Tatiana Woodly

He did not die
He was not sitting in a rocking chair
Or holding his family's hands
He did not go gently into the night
Or get to live a full life
HE WAS ASSASSINATED

He did not die
He stood for causes he held dear
His voice was loud, his stance was clear
He faced the storm with peril in sight
His spirit shone with unwavering light
HE WAS ASSASSINATED

He did not die
He remains in echoes and in dreams
In every voice that dares to speak
A legacy that will not fade
His ideals, forever laid
HE WAS ASSASSINATED

And he will never be forgotten

Authors

ISABELLA BALLEW won 1st Place of the Fiction Writing Contest. She is an emerging writer who currently lives in New York City. She is a designer by trade, and a writer and mixed-media artist after 5 o'clock. She currently cohabitates with one human (good) and two felines (evil).
Page 7

MEL EINHORN won 1st Place of the Poetry Writing Contest. Haunted by insistent sensations, intrigued by streams of consciousness, the poet considers estrangement, emancipation, high respect, great esteem.
Page 32

LENA N. GEMMER won 1st Place of the Non-Fiction Writing Contest. She is a multimedia artist originally from the quiet foggy town of Montara, CA. She received her BA in English and History from Allegheny College in Meadville PA, and her MFA in Writing from University of New Hampshire. Her work has been published in *Wild Roof Journal, Burningword Literary Journal, The Bangalore Review*, among others. When she is not in graduate school pursuing a PhD in English CW at SUNY Binghamton, you can find her taking photographs or scolding her Norwegian Forest cat, Mitchy.
Page 39

G. B. CROISSANT won 2nd Place of the Fiction Writing Contest. She is a part-time teacher, stay-at-home mom, and self-proclaimed "master of Latin." She has a Bachelor's Degree in Creative Writing with Honors from NAU. She lives in Mesa, Arizona, with her husband, toddler son, three absurd cats, and

a dog who pretends to be a cat.
Page 55

RJ BEE is a high school math teacher, and runs a podcast called the Helping Friendly Podcast, which focuses on music and storytelling; and a podcast called Library Card, which focuses on discussions of books and short stories. He lives in Merion Station, PA, just outside of Philadelphia.
Page 224

MARLOWE BLAIRE.
Page 101

PETER CASHORALI is a neurodivergent queer psychotherapist, formerly working in HIV/AIDS and community mental health, currently in private practice in Portland and Los Angeles.
Page 203

A J DALTON is a UK-based writer. He's published the *Empire of the Saviours* trilogy with Gollancz Orion, *The Satanic in Science Fiction and Fantasy* with Luna Press, the *Dark Woods*

Rising poetry collection with Starship Sloane, and other bits and bobs. He lives with his monstrously oppressive cat named Cleopatra.
Page 273; 275; 276

BLAKE EDWARDS is a Black writer from Lawrence, Massachusetts. He focuses on literary fiction, creative nonfiction, and screenwriting. Themes central in his work are death, sex, addiction, violence, masculinity, mental health, family, and dark romance. He currently lives in Los Angeles, California.
Page 204

MICHAEL EYRE writes poems. A number of his pieces have been published in literary magazines or been highly commended in poetry competitions. He is a graduate of Liverpool University and the University of Central Lancashire.
Page 201; 202

DANIEL FREARS is a UK native that has been

residing in New Zealand for close to 10 years. He produces short stories, prose and poetry. He has had short prose and poetry pieces published in The Spinoff, Salient, Quick Brown Dog, Shabby Doll House, Pulp and miniMAG and his short stories feature in CRAFT literary, Northridge Review and Roi Fainéant with further publications upcoming.
Page 106

KAVITHA REDDY GOYAL was born in India and raised in Ireland and the northeastern US. She recently retired from a thirty-year career in medicine and pharmaceutical research and is turning to a life-long dream of writing, with work on a novel. She is a wife and mother of two adult daughters, and makes her home in the Philadelphia area, where she enjoys nature and the arts.
Page 260

SAWYER HUNTER.
Page 121

JEFFERY JOHNSON is a retired professor of philosophy and an aspiring mystery and short story writer.
Page 178

DONNA LORMAND is a fiction writer originally from Louisiana, which we can all agree is the best state. She loves the sound of cicadas singing on summer nights and draws inspiration from the quiet, strange corners of everyday life. In her free time, she snuggles cats and pretends to be athletic. Her other work has been published in *After Dinner Conversation.*
Page 252

JOHN MARTINEZ is an aspiring young writer from central New Jersey looking to explore the way we interact with base desires and outward appearances.
Page 122

LARENA NELLIES-ORTIZ is a writer and photographer based in Oakland, California. Her work explores the intersections between people and place; memory and belonging. Her photography has been featured in The Sun Magazine, Barren Magazine, The Ilanot Review and Stonecoast Review, among others.

JOHN CHRISTOPHER NELSON is a graduate of the Stonecoast MFA and earned his BA in Literature from UCLA. His work is featured in *Chiron Review, Able Muse, The New Guard, Euphemism, The Blotter, Every Day Fiction, The Real Story*, and elsewhere.

RILEY PHILLIPS.

JOHN RC POTTER is an international educator from Canada, currently residing in Istanbul. He has experienced a revolution (Indonesia), air strikes (Israel), earthquakes (Turkey), boredom (UAE), and blinding snow blizzards (Canada), the last being the subject of his story, 'Snowbound in the House of God' (*Memoirist*). The author's poems, stories, essays, articles, and reviews have been published in various magazines and journals.

ROWAN QUINN.

MICHAEL ROQUE was born and raised in Los Angeles, Michael Roque discovered his love for poetry and prose amid friends on the bleachers of Pasadena City College. Now he currently lives in the Middle East and is being inspired by the world around him. His poems have been published by literary magazines like North Dakota Quarterly, Cholla Needles, The Literary Hatchet and others.

KURT SCHMIDT is the author of one novel, "Annapolis Misfit," (Crown Publishers, 1974) and the chapbook memoir, "Birth of a Risk-Taker," (Bottlecap Press, 2025). Anxiously, he flew in a plane piloted by his newly-licensed son. That story appeared in The Boston Globe.

Page 163

MICHAEL J. SHEPLEY a writer who lives and works in Sacramento, CA.

Page 93

T. B. VITTINI is a poet and librarian based in Sydney. His poetry has appeared in *Portside Review, Jacaranda Journal*, and *Trash to Treasure Lit.*

Page 104; 271

HOLLY AMBER WEBB is the author of two self-published poetry books titled *Am I the Villain?* and *From the River to the Sea: Poetry for a Free Palestine*. Her poetry has been featured in Permanent Answer Poetry Society's online 2025 magazine, and *Starcrossed Anthology: Volume One*, a collection published in 2023.

Page 98; 99

JACOB MICHALE WILLIAMS is a writer and self-described "midwestern boy", originally from St. Louis, Missouri. He is also a graduate of the MFA program at Memphis University. He specializes in fiction, as well as poetry and screenplays. In these genres, Jacob cannot help but write about family, memory, generational trauma, and the language of the subconscious.

Page 72

TATIANA WOODLY graduated from Northern Arizona University in 2022. She briefly worked with the Empyrean Literary Magazine in 2023.

Page 277

DOUGLAS YOUNG is an author and professor emeritus whose essays, poems, and short stories have appeared in a variety of publications in America, Canada, Europe, and Asia. His first novel, *Deep in the Forest*, was published in 2021 and the

second, *Due South*, came
out in 2022. His first book
of essays, *This Little
Opinion Plus $1.50 Will
Buy You a Coke*, appeared
in 2024, and the second,
Not Just Political, was
published in 2025.
Page 242

9 781957 960333